There Is This Place

Some elementary school connections are forever, and we help each other.

The bus stopped a block from the building and when Larry walked toward it he recognized an elementary school friend, Rita Owens, sitting on a bench under a covered bus stop. She was plainly dressed in shorts and a blouse, hair fluffed in a short afro style. Her eyes darted left and right as if she were waiting on someone, or afraid of someone. Larry thought to speak, or pass by without any acknowledgement, thinking that she probably wouldn't remember him anyway as she didn't seem present. Almost without her permission, as he got to within eight feet of her, he spoke her name from years ago, "Rita Owens."

She looked at him, as if from afar, sensing that he was okay, and knowing that he was okay, she responded, "Bishop. Rita Bishop. Miss Owens died several years ago."

She licked her lips and touched the middle of her chest, just over the heart, and repeated, "Bishop. Rita Bishop. Miss Owens died several years ago."

He looked at her, not knowing what to say, or do. He wanted to be polite but wasn't sure what was the next right action to take.

"You know the dream is dead; so, you need another dream. No one has said that. Stuck in the past. New dream, what it means. New dream." She spoke as if before a camera, clear, and with passion.

"You know the dream; you know the dream. They will ask you one day, and you will know the dream."

"Drugs, mental illness," he thought.

"Rita, my name is Larry..." Before he could complete the sentence, she began, "Fleming. Larry Fleming. Good boy. Got into those drugs and alcohol. Sex with everybody. Jail. Junkie man, alcoholic, dope fiend. Hoe. I saw you on TV, good boy returned. Good man now. No drugs, no alcohol. God boy. Good boy. Frankie overdosed last year. Kenny too. Ronnie Brown been in jail 12 years. Maureen wanted to come visit you, but she was going to trick you. She dead. My uncle is clean now, Johnny too. They married. Two men, but that's okay. How ya mama n 'em? They say I'm crazy. That's okay. I live back there."

She pointed to a spot 200 yards east of the building, past an open, park like area with nice trees and shrubbery.

"Not in the woods. Daddy left me the house. The men, the ones who made the Mears building new wanted to buy it. Then wanted to take it when I wouldn't sell. "Thirty thousand," they said, "Thirty thousand." Where I'm gone live, they didn't say? Daddy had worked for some people who helped me keep the house. Money now for the rest of my life. Kept daddy's house. Larry the counselor, good man now, new dream, new dream now."

"Rita," Larry spoke.

"I'm going now. You go to work. New dream, new dream. You tell them."

With that she stood, walked past Larry, and didn't look back.

Chapter Two

Thomas Robinson learned about computers on the Tang machines back in 1974. Quadratic equations and linear programming came easily to him and working in the Decision Mathematics Department gave him access to brilliant minds and high energy trials. Dr. Leopard, department head, was patient with him, and so clear in his explanations. Drs. Peters and Banner allowed him to read their work, and he saw their calculations as a bridge to mechanical applications.

He went to work for the Atlanta Police Department in 1978 and seemed to have an innate ability to project intuition and probability onto encounters with the public. His formulated thoughts per second were such that he saved a few lives, cops, and potential victims, by sensing intent, or lack thereof, versus a real threat. One case that stands out was the night he and three other detectives rode up on Simpson and Ashby and noticed Gary and Ken Hughley standing around slinging dope. They had files on their activities the past two years and neither warranted much attention, although Gary was moving into a crime level that was bigger than just his nickel and dime hustling to support his habit. He was carrying guns now, and his friends were moving ounces at a time.

When Thomas exited the unmarked police car and chased after him he figured Gary was either armed, or at least had a syringe with needle on him. Thomas knew from reports today, from six stores, that Gary was involved in the theft of at least 90 pairs of sunglasses, his primary hustle these days. When Gary ran past Kenny, who threw 16 glassine bags into the air and turned left behind Nate's Hot Dog Store, he started to reach for his right leg pants cuff. Thomas could see that and so as he chased and turned the corner behind him he could see Gary's arm moving downward, then relax as if he'd thrown something atop the building. As Thomas drew his weapon a split-second decision was on him, is he armed, or was that something else? Fortunately for both Gary turned, with hands above his head, as Thomas had already decided not to shoot. That is when he got the idea for Weapons Eye Sync and was able to 'see' how valuable it would be if law enforcement had a device that could tell them if, and with what type of weapon subjects had on them, and their level of intention to do harm from at minimum teyards away. He developed a basic concept, and made some drawings, and acquired a patent, # 661454332190. Ten years later he left the police force, took a job at Hobe Phone Company as a Systems Flow Designer, and that is where he met, and became familiar with the work of Bruce Walker, who had come over from Atlanta Scientific as a System Performance Analyst. They worked together on the company's top five projects for eight years and were then disbursed to top secret jobs in either research or training for the next twelve years. They retired from there in June 2008.

*

Funny how a movement affects an area, and an area affects a movement. The hardscrabble, blue-collar nature of the area near the Mears building had become home to the homeless, playground for the tricksters, and a focus for the aimless. The Atlanta Crackers baseball field was long gone, the Army recruiting office boarded up, and drunks were everywhere. Yet, there was a glamour to it all, a halo of night lights, clothes, and artist not yet distinguished, 24-hour eating places, and flop houses for the girls. The races had merged, and were getting to know each other, and north side businesses still paid the bills. Achievement mattered, and rural attitudes shaped the burgeoning urban landscape, "Yes sir, and No ma'am," could still be heard, and dating for pleasure was often the norm. High school and cars would state the obvious, compact, or large still meant something. The creeks and trussells and railroad tracks defined the places you should not go, or better yet, you had to explore. Cathy and Jeanie would come outside, cigarettes and wine could be bought, another day, another time.

*

Larry's ego wanted to present a better front even though his office was tasteful, with modern art and furnishings purchased by Darlene that could be resold later if necessary. Larry was a good counselor. He was well respected, but felt small at times because he, even as a young boy, thought that all his play mates had a dollar more than he had, that they went places, and did things, while he seemed always to be just out and about, running around, playing sports, spending money given to him by his aunts. He didn't seem to know how to make money like his uncles, but he cut the grass, or cleaned off roofs, painted houses and inside rooms. People knew they could depend on him, even as his bad years progressed he could be called on for small repairs and jobs the other young folks were not doing, at least in his neighborhood.

"Come in. Mr. Henson?"

"Yes, hi, Wallace Henson. Good morning. Good to meet you. Nelson spoke highly of you."

"Thank you. Yes, come on in, have a seat."

Wallace was having second thoughts about all of this. Maybe he was overreacting to his latest drinking spree, but his business woes were very real and foreboding. He thought he'd overpaid for the Weapons Eye Sync device and had borrowed way too much to finance the deal. Sure, the return potential was enormous, but he felt that his management skills were not strong enough to take the company to the next level. He would have to confide more in Jake about the deal but didn't want to corrupt the young man any more than he had already. Wallace thought he knew the racial politics and thought he could avoid the consequences of what Mr. Robinson's true motives were for the device's future. So, coming to talk to an older, black counselor from Atlanta, Georgia seemed appropriate on many levels.

"How is Nelson these days?" Larry asked, taking a seat, then gesturing towards a bottle of water and coffee pot. "Water, coffee?"

"No thanks," Wallace responds. "He's not well. Late-stage cancer. Bad."

Larry places his face in his upturned hands. "Well," he says under his breath.

They both shift in their chairs, eye one another with caution, let out a deep breath, then Larry asks him, "What can I do for you?"

Wallace was taken aback by the question, expecting more small talk about their mutual friend.

"Well, I'm not sure. I know you're primarily an addiction counselor, and I do have some issues there, but I have some other needs that may be related or not. Issues around business and social consciousness. I may have done something to hurt a lot of people where I wanted to be helpful. Good motive, potentially bad results."

"My general consults are $400.00. Then we'll see where we go from there."

"Sure, fine. Do I pay you now?"

"Let's get that out of the way first."

Wallace writes him a check for the amount, Larry offers a receipt. "That won't be necessary," Wallace says.

"You were born and raised here I understand?" Wallace asks.

"Yeah, sure. 1953. Grady Baby."

"What does that mean?"

"It means my roots are deep here."

"And you, where are you from?"

"New York actually. Just outside the city. Upper middle, neat, comfortable."

"Family?"

"Okay, let me tell you what's really going on," Wallace exhorts, and begins to sweat. "Those bastards want to kill me! But I want to get them first, business wise I mean. They look good on TV. Talking all that stuff. Chumps!" He's breathing heavily now, looking around the room, restless. He gets up, walks over to the table, and grabs the bottle of water. Screws the top off and returns to his seat. "I'm sorry. I messed up. Those bastards."

He takes a gulp of water, and looks directly at Larry, and asks, "You got something to drink around here?"

Larry walked up the two flights of stairs for his 11 o'clock massage with Teresa. He felt good that he didn't have any major body ailments that needed work. It had been a year and a few months since he emptied Aunt Cadelia's house to prepare for sale. He'd wrenched his right shoulder moving a refrigerator, strained both knees moving old metal desks, wooden boards, and shelving from the basement, and had fallen down the front porch steps moving a four-drawer filing cabinet, breaking the big toe of his left foot. Golf had stressed his lower back and clearing bushes and trees at his house had aggravated his whole body, especially inflaming the shoulders, forearm, and knees. His left heel showed signs of plantar fasciitis, and his feet generally hurt all day. OTC anti-inflammatory medications had kept him going, but four tablets a day were doing harm to his stomach, causing him to overeat. He'd not had a massage in six months and most of the ailments had healed so he looked forward to today's session.

Teresa, already a full-sized black woman at 5'8" 180lbs. looked as if she'd gained weight, sitting at the front desk, shoulders and face much fuller since the last time he saw her. She welcomed him warmly, seeming to not remember him, having to glance at her appointment book before speaking further, "Larry?"

"Yes. How are you?"

"Good. It's been a while," she speaks.

"Yes."

"Come on back."

She gets up and leads him down a short hallway saying, "Room 3."

"On the left?"

"No, on the right."

She gestures there, and he goes into the room.

The massage table was neatly wrapped with a sheet, and the top blanket folded back. The support pillow for the knees was evident, and the room was comfortably warm. The lighting was soft and gentle on the senses, just like the music.

"Go ahead and get ready, face down first," she offered. "I'll be back shortly."

"Okay," he responds.

Larry put his phone on silent, removes his tee and over shirt, put his socks in his shoes, right to right, left to left, and pushes them under the chair. He removes his pants, folding the clothes on the chair before sitting on the table. He slowly leaned sideways, then face down, positioning his face in the cradle, and gently shifting his face and body to get comfortable. It took several times to get his face comfortable, and to move his legs and arms to a resting position. He casually thought how good this felt and blinked his eyes a few times before closing them. Teresa returned in three minutes, just before Larry was beginning to question to himself how long it would be before she returned. She gently tapped on the closed door and came in, not hearing his response.

"Ready?" she had asked.

She moved to his left side and asked, "What are we working on today?"

"Just a general massage with some attention to my right shoulder," he answered.

She walked around the massage table, turned to the short, square cabinet that housed her supplies, picked out a jar of cream, and opened it. She asked if the room, blanket, and pad felt okay; he said yes. She then stepped backwards, then moved towards him, pushing his body at various points, waist, legs, hips, arms, shoulders. She touched his feet and jostled his ankles. She used her fingers on his back, pushing, sensing, probing, as Larry's mind became more active.

He thought of his last counseling session, and whether the guy would ever get honest about how much he drinks. He knew from past experiences that in a group setting it usually took about four sessions, but in individual people could minimize for weeks, choosing to talk about peripheral problems because they didn't have the benefit of older group members who were more comfortable with the process.

As the massage progressed Larry was able to mentally satisfy a few techniques to use for his next two clients later in the day, a lawyer, and a businessman. Teresa had touched a couple of sensitive areas, but generally there were no 'ouhwee' moments. He acknowledged to himself how powerful she was, yet, with just the right amount of force.

When she was nearing the end of the hour Larry asked if she had refined some of her previous techniques, observing that she seemed more in command of her huge talents.

"Oh," she paused, "Thanks. We do have to take classes to maintain our licenses. I like the hands-on classes, not just online, which we can have one half of. Thanks, I appreciate that," she responded.

"Oh yeah, my whole body feels comfortable now. Good not to have sore points that really needed attention."

As he dressed and checked his phone he had a feeling of satisfaction. He was glad they talked of allowing enough time to heal, and how this massage came at the perfect time for him to assess his body's power to correct past indulgencies given proper care and rest.

He went to the front desk, paid the $80.00 fee, and gave her a $15.00 tip.

"Thank you," he said. "I'll get back with you."

"All right. Don't let it be so long next time. And thank you."

He grabbed the bottle of water set on top of the desk for him, grabbed a few mints from a bowl, and walked out the front door.

###

Larry was born in 1953 to Doug and Martha Fleming. Larry was a healthy 8.5lbs at birth. He was loved and nurtured from the start as he was Martha's first born. Her three sisters and one brother showed much love to Larry, and support for the new family, especially Tina, the oldest sister. Tina was firm and sure, and guided many aspects of diaper changes and wash, bedding, clothing, and general holding, feeding, and singing to the handsome baby boy. Even their friends and neighbors seemed drawn to this child in a special way helping where needed, someone always coming over to their small apartment on Sunrise Street, a mile away from her parent's house.

Martha met Doug after they graduated from high school. She started college at Spelman, and he worked for Cooper's Drug Store down the street. She and a girlfriend stopped by one afternoon to get a Freezy and Doug made it up for them. He took a liking to Martha right away as she seemed a bit shy and reserved. They all talked while Doug worked to sweep up and move stuff around, and Martha couldn't keep her eyes away from his movements. She liked how funny he could be, and how he seemed to have a special smile for her on the days she came to the store.

He asked her out for a movie at Bailey's Theater and paid the fifteen cents for her ticket. After a while she became pregnant, left school, and took a job at the Needham factory. They married, rented the apartment on Sunrise, and lived there through the birth of their second son, Leroy. Doug started gambling and winning a lot of money at cards and the numbers, was arrested twice, and left town by the time Larry turned five, and Leroy was four. Martha moved back in with her family, returned to college, and earned a degree in education. Doug would call occasionally, but they never got back together. She got a job with the school system and moved to her own place when the boys were nine and ten.

###

"No, I don't have anything stronger here. If you need to go out and get something and come back another day that's fine."

"I'm just a little upset. I've spent my whole life doing good things well and now this. Excuse me for the profanity, I'm just really baffled how I was framed. I didn't see it coming. Man, those guys set me up. Money, I guess; I was blinded by the billionaire thing. Didn't need it of course. Billionaire."

Henson returned to his seat and asked for more water.

"Sure," Larry responded.

"So how do we do this, way back or recent history?"

"Recent. Remember, I'm a counselor, not a business guru or doctor," spoken with a wry smile.

"All right counselor," Henson spoke, taking his suit coat off, "here we go."

He searched the walls and noticed the certified addiction counselor documents, and several articles that said this guy knew his craft. Still, he wasn't sure if he wanted to go through with this conversation.

"Let's start here: In 1997 I pulled off the deal of a lifetime. I'd made some moves, but this was almost too good to be true. I'm a numbers guy, right, and a friend of a friend needed some tax help for his growing electronics business. He had developed a semiconductor that was revolutionary, and was making money hand over fist, as the saying goes. I don't know, well I guess I can tell you the details now, let's just say he personally earned $200,000,000.00 in 1996. He had missed a patent deadline, resolved that, but the whole process of running the company, blah, blah, blah had burned him out and he was ready to sell. I put together a package, bought it, patents, plans, customers, etc. for $120,000,000.00."

Henson starts to laugh to himself, then says with bravado, "I didn't have to pull a weapon!" He laughs uncontrollably for a few seconds, then composes himself.

"As is my custom, I worked very hard for eleven years and grew the business and have shared a lot of profit with the people who have been with me and worked just as hard. All very rich now as well," he says very calmly.

"It all sounds pretty wonderful so far," Larry remarks.

"Well, it took turn for the worse."

When Thomas and Bruce retired from Hobe in June 2008 they talked of the work they'd done there, and how rewarding it had been. The technological equipment they played with was truly amazing, though certain aspects of the research into behavior and intentionality felt wrong. They had given the company their best efforts and were proud of what they accomplished. Thomas was especially proud that he had not mentioned Weapons Eye Sync to anyone. He felt comfortable enough with Bruce's level of expertise and moral fiber to broach the idea of becoming his partner in business, and further develop his idea. Thomas invited Bruce to come to his house on September 30 to discuss an idea he'd been kicking around a few years. Bruce agreed and arrived about 7:15pm.

"Come in."

Bruce comfortably crossed the front threshold.

"Good evening. Nice evening; still warm."

"Yes, come on in; we'll go to the den. Drink?"

"No, I'm fine, thanks."

"Bruce how are you this evening?" Shirley asks as she comes to give him a hug. "Good to see you: how's Mary?"

"Good, she's good. She says hello."

"When are we all going to get together for dinner and a movie?"

"Soon, let's do it soon."

"Tell her to call me and we'll make some plans."

"I'll do it."

Bruce smiles to her as he moves on to the den through the kitchen. Thomas follows him and closed the door behind them.

"Wow can't believe it's been four months!" Thomas starts.

"Yeah, we had a good trip to Arizona. Very relaxing. Sedona, the Canyon; just all over was nice."

"Three weeks?" Thomas asks, yet really confirming what he already knew.

"Right, yeah, great."

"Well," Thomas pauses, "I asked you over to discuss a business proposal. Something you know a lot about and like what we worked on at Hobe. It's something I developed after leaving the police force back in '88. It has to do with weapon recognition, and a perpetrator's abilities to harm law enforcement personnel."

"Sounds exciting."

"Well it is, with a potential to help the good guys, and make us a lot of money. I need you because of your performance control work, how you've uncovered flaws in otherwise foolproof systems. I don't want to discuss too much tonight, and we can go over particulars at another time."

"Yeah, I'm open."

"Good. Tomorrow too soon?"

"Not at all. Early is good."

"8a?"

"Sure. Here?"

"Yeah. 8a. See you in the morning."

"Okay!"

Bruce says goodnight to Shirley and almost floats out the door.

Chapter Three

Jack Moran was the lead person for the special weapons division of Hobe Phone Company, the government's research arm into behavior and intentionality. Its purpose was to study 'How Our Brothers Evolved,' an ongoing thesis concerned with the peculiar connections between American blacks and whites. They had spent years with the whole White versus Caucasian models, but now the quest had been to resolve the notion that black people from south of the Sahara in Africa, years later, required different systems to penetrate a variance in moral structure. Skin color was the main driver of the studies, but the realities of Caucasians from North Africa, Somalia, or Arabs and some people from India confused the narrow boundaries so far. When Thomas Robinson was recruited in 1986 he had already solved certain issues of physical integrity using sound wave variance, but what he was charged with now to develop was a little scary.

Thomas hired 20 actors for today's skin color recognition tests that Jack had ordered. They ranged from pale white to deep black. He was convinced their sensors could not only detect motives by skin color, but also degrees of intent of a possible crime suspect. Using historical data, he was curious about whether weight and spatial filters could influence translation algorithms. He knew that defined variance could be put into mathematical formulae, but would the device accept changes in brain/body signals?

There were two teams of ten each who were assigned various roles, white normal to dark skin normal, with cultural nuance factored in, i.e., levels of industry, perception of freedom, achievements, expectations, and heritage. These were mixed with propensity for criminal behaviors, and how they were defined by each sub-group. Other indicators were capacity for learning, meaning comprehension, and knowledge of performance parameters. IQ and morality would be assigned and codified later.

The control group would define how the device functioned with basic, old-school intentions. With the test group could it adapt to mixed use motives? The results would show how certain skin color groups define work for hire as a sociological requisite, drug dealing, or identity fraud, for instance. Could the scanning sensor discern accepted procedure, and identify intent, skill level, and the type weapon carried by the individual, all in .82 seconds? This was the stated goal of these tests.

Darlene Jackson enjoyed a good corporate career with the airlines. She worked in HR as an executive trainer and was well regarded in her tight network. She was tall and healthy, working out twice a week, casually dating other professionals, and collected black themed art. She had a master's in social work, and always received excellent yearly reviews for her work performance. She was making $94,000.00 a year when she met Larry. She owned a split-level home in Stone Mountain's West Street community and drove a standard sedan. At 43 years old, she would still be called cute, and had a good, positive circle of girlfriends who met regularly for dinner. All of them were still single, or divorced, so the conversation usually covered four topics: men, finance, travels, and social commentary. Tonight's conversation was about good black men who'd served prison time, and about their age, and whether they should consider dating any?

"What about your brother?" Paula asked Joyce Taylor as Darlene listened intently.

"You know, Ronnie was so good growing up; decent, smart, athletic, family oriented. It was a mild shock when he got busted," Joyce shared.

"What do you mean 'mild'?" Darlene asked.

"Bank Fraud. He covered up so well. He wasn't flashy. We thought he was following suit, working hard, taking classes, getting coached. We just thought all that was paying off well for him."

"What happened?" Darlene followed up, noticing Joyce tense up and withdraw a bit.

"All he said was he was helping some dancers at Johnny's club buy their first homes," Joyce responded.

"How much time?" Paula asked.

"96 months."

"Federal?"

"Yes," Joyce answered.

"When does he get out?" Paula further probes.

"Two months. He's in a half-way house now," Joyce gives them.

"Have y'all gone to see him there?"

"Sure. You want to see him?" Joyce asked Paula.

They all gave a laugh.

"Darlene, didn't you date him one time?" Paula asked.

"Don't even start there!" Darlene shot back.

They all laugh again.

These were five good, fine, black ladies who had lived right, gone to school, and had positive social and family lives. Now, starting middle age, they were honestly searching for the other pieces of their lives.

###

Darlene was introduced to Larry by a mutual friend. They talked a few times by phone and made plans for dinner and to attend a Philosophy Society Lecture afterwards if all was going well. They agreed to meet at a small restaurant near Grady Park at 6 on Saturday September 24, 1998. The lecture was only two miles away.

She arrived first and parked near the front entrance. Larry arrived and parked a few spaces away, closer to the street. They greeted each other warmly and went in.

"Thanks for coming," spoke David, the chef owner who greeted them.

"We're glad to be here," spoke Larry. "Rich told me to tell you hello."

"Richie Cooper?" questioned David.

"Yeah. Good friend."

"Yes, he is. How's his wife, Christine?" asked David.

"Good. Good. Her surgery went well."

"Such good people," David shared.

"How about over here, window view of the park?"

"Looks great," Darlene spoke up as she looked towards Larry.

"Sure, looks good to me," Larry offered.

David gestured to the adequately sized table for two, assisted Darlene with her chair and nodded to Larry.

"Thanks," Larry and Darlene said in unison.

"Justin will be your waiter. Oh, here he is now."

Justin steps up to the table, smiles and says, "Hello."

David pauses, "I don't know your names," he says, a bit embarrassed.

"I'm Darlene, he's Larry."

"Thanks," David says, "My bad, okay. I'm going now. Justin will take good care of you."

David walks off quickly.

"Drinks?" Justin asks.

"Water, water," Larry and Darlene answer.

Justin asks, as he's giving them a menu, "First time here?"

"Yes," they each respond.

"Hopefully, you'll have a good experience. We're quite proud of what we do here."

'We've heard good things," Larry responds.

"Okay, make yourselves comfortable, and I'll return in a few minutes with your waters."

"Thank you," Larry again responds.

Since it was still warm for late September Darlene was tastefully dressed in a light sweater. Larry was casual with khaki slacks, open collar dress shirt and a suit coat.

"This seems nice," Darlene observes.

"Yeah," Larry asserts.

They each fumble nervously while reading the menus.

"Well here we are," Darlene starts.

"Shrimp, scallops okay?" Larry asks.

"Sure," she answers.

"Thanks again for agreeing to this."

"Sure. I needed to get out."

"Why is that?" he asks.

"Work's been busy lately with 20 new hires, and I've had to train them all in phase one; introductions, rules, ethics, SOPs, all that before they get to their workstations."

"Sounds hectic?"

"Just busy; four hours of that each day then my other work. But I enjoy it. I want to prepare them for our work culture, and I want to be as thorough as possible."

"I'm sure."

"Well I think you have to give people your best. This is where they form notions about what's to come and what's expected of them, as well as what we give. I want them to know why we're successful, and what they'll need to do to add to the growth of the company. Of course, we've screened them, checked their resumes, accomplishments, other histories, drug tests, criminal background checks, etc. We're not social services."

"Wow, I probably couldn't get a job there," Larry says, jokingly.

"Naaahhh, you're fine; I know who you are."

"Oh, you checked me out?" he asks.

"Somewhat. You'll have to fill in a few gaps," she laughs. "How about me, what do you know?"

"Vanilla, or rather chocolate chip. What you see is what you get."

"That's kind of you."

They laugh a bit longer, and shyly eye each other for a few seconds.

"Here we go. I brought some lemon slices just in case you'd want to add them to your water," Justin announces.

"How thoughtful," Darlene says.

"How would y'all like to start," he asks, setting their waters on paper coasters, and placing the lemon wedges in the center of the table on a small glass dish.

"Shrimp, scallops, a crab cake we can split," Larry orders, looking directly at Darlene.

She nods okay.

"Sure. I'll get that right out. Questions about dinner choices?"

"Not yet. Thanks," they answer.

Darlene thinks Larry is a good-looking man. "So far, he seems okay," she thinks, as she studies his actions.

###

Rita seemed glad to see Larry this afternoon. He was walking fast and didn't have time to spare. It was five thirty and his group started at six.

She was fully dressed in a coat and a woolen cap on her head. She was rocking back and forth, sitting on the bench, a fast-food bag to her left, crumpled as if the food had been eaten, and the wrapping paper, or an empty carton was inside. Larry knew he had to make time for her, so he walked towards her.

"Counselor," she almost shouted to him.

"Hey Rita," he greeted her.

"Your granddaddy lived near here too, over on Irwin Street. Your grandmamma and two kids. He was a great man too. Wise. Wise. You are great, you know? Tell them about the new dream."

"Rita, I've got to..."

"6 o'clock. I know. But don't be afraid, old man dream needs to rest. New dream. Tell them about the new dream."

"Thank you, Rita."

She smiles, away from him as he walks off to the office.

*

Four people were standing outside Larry's office door when he stepped off the elevator. He smiled, slowed his pace, and greeted them.

"Hey y'all. Let me get to the door here."

He puts his key into the cylinder, turns to open it and steps inside. He turns on the overhead lights, walks over to a lamp on the main table, turns it on, turns around and says, as his clients start in, "Come over here, I'll get you signed in."

He sits at the table, pulls a sign in sheet from a folder, retrieves a pen and a receipt book from the drawer, and starts taking the $60.00 fee from each one: "Name, probation officer, 1st or 2nd DUI, or other offense," he questions, as he takes the money, writes down their name and other information, stacks the money in a pile in front of him, makes change if necessary, or says he'll give it to them later. They line up, and one by one he signs them in as seven others show up before six.

"Have a seat in the group room," he announces, "We'll start in a few minutes. I'll pass out receipts at the end of group."

They all take seats, talk amongst themselves, and wait for Larry to come back.

The group room, like the reception area, had beautiful watercolor pictures on the walls. Two were fall scenes, two were beach scenes, and one was like an outdoor snapshot from New Mexico, hills, and a valley near the Rio Grande somewhere. The chairs are high back-office types on casters, and you could move around or stay set in one place.

"Okay, let's get started," Larry announces. "My name is Larry Fleming, Certified Addiction Counselor, and I'm glad to see everybody, but I'm sure most of you are not happy to be here. I try to teach and entertain, and I hope you'll get more out of this than just your letter of completion. That depends on you. The rules are simple; listen, talk, respect each other, get honest, and grow up a little bit. I'm a counselor, not your probation officer. The legal stuff is on you, whether you did it or not that's for you and the courts. What we talk about here is addiction, alcoholism, or bullshit; you lie to me, I'll lie to you. I'm a dope fiend. I was out there for eighteen years if you've done it I probably did it too. One difference is I've been clean and sober 28 years now and have a pretty good life. It's what you want to do about your problem. How it works is I'll probably talk the first hour, you talk the second hour, and then we'll all talk the third hour. Sometimes we'll watch an educational video, sometimes a movie. This is not 'AA,' or any other 'A,' people who go there want to be there, you've been forced to come, and pay; those are free services. But, if you are an addict, or alcoholic, or just pretending, you already know. I've been at this a long time and some of what you are going to say I'll think it's crazy, and some of what I say you'll think it's crazy. Hopefully, at the end of three hours we've all learned something about ourselves, or someone else."

*

All fidget a little, adjust their seated positions, and take a breath.

"Now, I generally don't like profanity, but I will go 'ghetto' if I have to. We're not going to argue too long about anything. I will call the police, quick, if a real threat is made. Like I said, respect, civility, and we will have classes on those topics." Larry takes a deep breath. "Okay, let's do the question-and-answer thing. First, let's go around the room and introduce ourselves. We'll start to my left and go around the room. State your name, and why you're here. All right let's start here," he gestures to his left.

"My name is Lester Ross, 2nd DUI."

"My name is Sharon Fuller, drug possession."

"My name is Robert Thompson, theft by taking."

"I'm Johnny, I'm just here man," he says, as the group laughs.

"I'm Tori Davis, solicitation."

"My name is Doris Jones, DUI."

"I'm Sarah, pot."

"I'm Joan, heroin addict, theft."

"Davis, public indecency, pot."

"Mr. James Harris, alcohol consumption."

"Gina Rawlings, gave cop a blow job."

The group bursts out in laughter for a few seconds.

From the individual evaluations sent over to him, and the couple that he had done, the average age of the group was 24, seven were high school graduates, two dropped out, and one had a GED. Doris Jones was a professor in African American Literature. None of these clients had done hard prison time, although three had served nine months in County. Most had been arrested, sent to probation, and the courts had ordered substance abuse counseling. Larry knew this population well and looked forward to each group session.

After group, walking up to the bus stop, Larry thought of his nine-month tour of duty with the 4th Infantry Division in West Germany in 1973. He remembered thinking he not only let his Uncle Lewis down, who soldiered on German soil during WWII, but Generals Frank O. Davis, Jr. and Sr., men who distinguished themselves there as well, in the air and on the land. Men who beat segregation by their performance, beat it by determination, sacrifice, and a will to excel. Jr., who led the Tuskegee Airmen to unparalleled success with their escort missions, meeting several German FW-190s and ME 262 jet aircraft, destroying several, and damaging others, showed that black men too had the good stuff, dignity, precision, and reserve. Larry thought how they would not have approved of how he relieved himself of any moral fortitude, had resigned any mental agility, had become, by his abuse of drugs, a low life, unworthy of any mention of having once been a military man, though to his credit he did perform several top-secret missions that were successful; two sanctioned, one not.

It took three months for Thomas and Bruce to get the business structure in place. They had to hire a law firm, accountants, a sales force, consultants for trade laws governing foreign commerce, and general office staff. They found out about the Mears building in downtown Atlanta and leased about 10,000 square feet for three years. There had been much discussion about the location, and they decided here their clients would get a good view of the city driving in from Hartsfield-Jackson, or an outlying smaller airport. They figured, rightly, that most of the buyers they were after would come by private jet anyway, and have limousines bring them to the office from there.

Of course, Thomas Robinson, owner, was designated CEO, and Bruce Walker was given 20% of the company, and named COO. By December 2008 they were fully operational.

*

The people who had been following Mr. Henson now followed Larry Fleming. They couldn't understand why Mr. Henson came to Mr. Fleming's office each Tuesday at 2pm. They knew Fleming was a substance abuse counselor of some distinction, but Henson had no known addiction issues. Today, warm, and sunny, Larry was out for an early morning jog through his neighborhood and the two spies knew their cover had been blown, that his pattern was different, and that he took a call for the first time in 20 runs over the past two months. It was Wallace Henson.

"Hey Wallace, how are you?"

"Fine, look, can we move our session to noon today?"

"Sure. See you then."

"Okay, thanks."

Wallace hung up and turned to the young woman next to him.

"Okay, that's done. What's next?" he asks her.

Sally Penfield was a Mergers and Acquisitions specialist with White, Farmer, and White. They were helping Henson with the purchase of Weapons Eye Sync, and some patent issues.

"So, will I own them or not, and can we buy the company?" he asks her.

"You will own them. Mr. Robinson had done some work for Hobe Phone Company and they're maintaining he stole some of their technology. He says he'd already developed that type sensor and had a patent for it. In his work for them they wanted a modified version of a chip for not only the skin color detection capability, but also the IQ component. That's what he and Mr. Walker created for them. Robinson's earlier chip was primarily about intent of action. Robinson and Walker have always said when they left Hobe they left that work there because it was work for hire. Mr. Robinson had produced sketches, dates, patent numbers, and certified copies of his invention. Plus, Blintel Corporation was way ahead of them both in those departments. Their stuff goes back to the 70s. We have a court date January 19, 2012. Thomas and Bruce have signed depositions and will not have to appear for us, or the other side; they've been ruled neutral."

"That's not good; we need them for our case, don't we?"

"The phone company wants the patents, not your money."

Henson laughs slightly.

The Supreme Court sided with Weapons Eye Sync, stating that the Federal Appeals Court wrongly overturned the lower court's ruling about the three patents. Weapons Eye Sync keeps its exclusive rights to the chip, and thus can go forward with a sale of the company.

Chapter Four

Mary and Shirley rode down to the office on Thursday to touch up the place. Most of the furnishings were in place, pictures hung, and art pieces set well on their stands. There was a good mix of wood, metal, and glass. Chairs were ergonomic, but not exotic, the ten-foot high ceilings gave the place an airy comfort. The modest sized individual offices were staged to welcome PCs, laptops, flip phones, and recreational listening devices. General staff was a good mix of military, law enforcement, educators, experienced administrative staff, and top sales professionals. The research department had physicists, psychologists, medical doctors, and a nurse; sometimes they outsourced testing, yet Bruce was highly skilled in design and quality control, so he would oversee any difficulties with the products they devised. He was hands on, but not intrusive.

Bruce and Thomas met the wives when they entered, standing at attention like two schoolboys who had won the science fair.

"Ladies, entrez-vous, sil vous plait," Bruce spoke up.

"Merci," both ladies responded as all chuckled.

"Come to preview the finished product?" Thomas followed, "Let's have a tour."

The ladies entered, professionally dressed in neat skirts, and well-fitting jackets over white blouses. They wore low heeled black shoes. Shirley was a striking blonde whose air of culture and refinement was in abeyance in this setting. She didn't need to prance around the work force. Mary, being more modest by nature, as well as Bruce, didn't have any airs to 'put on,' she was moderate with a warm smile. They'd all had enough years together in work and social settings to understand the strengths and vulnerabilities of each other. Both families were comfortable financially with the assurance that more big money was on the way. Plus, they all felt measured by their actions and not the money.

"Let's start in my office," Thomas presented, "Then we'll walk the track."

Track being the reference for the flow of the office's design, almost like an automobile assembly line, one part connects to the other part, start to finish.

###

History:

Wallace Henson, 63, male, CPA, intact family, two brothers, younger.

1970 Graduates Lakeside High School

1971-1973 US Army

1974 Married Sally Rogers. They have four children two girls, and two boys.

1977 Graduates University of Georgia; CPA 1979

1979-1989 Works for the IRS

1989 Opens CPA business with two employees: grosses $160,000.00

1991 Bought, then sold three investment properties (houses). Earned $30,000.00

1993 Bought, then sold eight investment properties (houses). Earned $110,000.00

1995 Bought receivables worth $800,000.00, repackaged, then sold for $600,000.00. Earned $200,000.00

1997 Bought Semi-Conductor Company with 32 employees.

1998 Incorporated Henson Technologies.

2011 Offers to buy Weapons Eye Sync

2012 Completes deal for WES

Wallace Henson 5/2012

"Like most of the people I know, I've worked hard and had good results. I've been blessed with good health, and at sixty-three I feel pretty good. I guess since the divorce I've not done well in relationships," Wallace was saying.

"Why do you think that's so?" Larry asks him.

"Well, if I'm honest, it could have something to do with my drinking. I can get mean towards women when I drink. Just a lot I didn't get to practice. I turned to business, and 'business relationships,' and I don't think I have a clue what it really means to be intimate with a woman."

"Anything steady now?"

"About four years ago. She was nice, and we did all the nice stuff, travel, movies, art stuff, dinners; you know."

"Had she moved in?"

"No. I'd sleep at her place, she at mine, but it lacked something."

"Any other kinds of relationships?" Larry asks without being direct.

"No, straight. No problems there. Like a friend says, I have trouble 'committing' to the relationship."

"Probably the booze. Let's see," Larry reaches behind him for Wallace's file, then reads softly, "15, starts drinking, tried pot, didn't like it, sniff or two of cocaine in college, modest drinking after college, out of control for a few months in '99, quit for two years, up and down since. Two steady relationships, one two years, one five. They broke off—, no ring. Heavy the last five months, suicidal. Suicidal?"

"Let's talk about that," Wallace jumps in.

"Take your time, this is big stuff. Where are you right now with that?" Larry asks cautiously.

"Nothing now. I wrote it down because when I got out of control sometimes, I'd really feel disgusted. Never a plan."

"Last drink?"

"Yesterday."

"Are you taking any medications?"

"Something for sleep sometimes."

"From a Doc?"

"OTC."

"How often?"

"Once, twice a week at times."

"What else?"

"That's it."

"Any drugs of abuse now, crack, meth, heroin on the weekends?" Larry smiles as he's asking.

"Not my style."

"How about some of your, umm, dates, girlfriends in the past?"

"Not even. They've been mostly the 'wine with dinner' types who otherwise don't drink, and don't finish those when ordered."

"So, are you a drunk?" Larry asks directly.

"Maybe. But what's going on now is the stress of buying this company. There are some social implications that are disturbing."

"How so?"

"Man, we don't have but a few minutes left; that answer is long."

"Okay, let's wrap up for today. Now tell me..."

Wallace interrupts.

"I used to hunt and target shoot, and I have two 'nines, an old school .38 for effect, and a rifle. If you say it, I'll give them to you, or Nelson, or whoever. If some clown tries to rob me so be it!"

"Your call."

"I'll keep them for now."

"The drinking?"

"I may need help with that."

"AA?"

"Twice. Not for me."

"How sick do you get when you try to stop. Vomiting, shakes, heart palpitations, sweats?"

"Some weakness and restlessness; no vomiting, no palpitations, some shakiness."

"High blood pressure?"

"It goes up. If I drink a lot of water and orange juice and eat something I'm usually all right."

"Call me tomorrow near noon whether you drink tonight or not."

"I won't drink, I'll have my friend come by and check on me. She's a trained nurse. I don't need a paper trail before closing this deal."

"What's most important?"

"I get that. I'll call tomorrow, and if you think we need to do something else I'll trust your decision."

"Does your friend know addiction medicine?"

"Psych nurse, Ledford a few years ago. She'll check my vitals. I'll give her your number. I don't want to die, and I do know I need help."

"Okay."

"How do you know all this? Nelson didn't say much except you're experienced?"

"Big problem back in the day. We'll talk more about me later. Stay safe, stay around."

"You're a comedian too?"

"Send in the clowns."

"Don't bother, they're here."

They have a good laugh, Wallace stands, looks Larry in the eyes and says, "Thanks."

Matthew Howard, MD, head of training for WES, wanted the R&D unit to hire a few minority temporary workers. He specified two African Americans, a Hispanic, and a Middle Easterner. Also, he mentioned that it would be helpful if they were recruited from a half-way house connected to federal inmates from prison. Plus, that they were at least 42 years old, and had been in prison since they were at least 24 years old, particularly crack dealers, as they would make the best subjects for study with the next phase of trials on the M2635 unit, intent versus motive.

*

Both Thomas and Shirley knew about secrets, she was thinking after the lecture. She had dated a black guy in college. He was nice and civil, and liked art and literature, and the race component gave the relationship a nice edge, but she was high octane, and he just didn't have the 'juice' to get her home, so to speak. Thomas was different, he was cordial, bright, and a liar. When they started dating he was already successful in his work, but when talking about his family he'd fudge a bit. It was only after a few more dates that he told her about Ron, his mentally challenged younger brother. He was not ashamed about the fact but was uncomfortable talking about it. She was not sure if she should ever mention Randall based on some comments Thomas made when they were out for a movie one Sunday afternoon.

"Probably a crack dealer," Thomas had commented, "What's a young black boy doing in a car like that!? I'm sure he's not a doctor."

"He could be," Shirley answered.

"No way. That one has not done a day of legal work in his life. Look how he's driving, parking like he owns the place. And I bet that white girl with him is a prostitute."

"Thomas, you're kidding. It's 1983. You're kidding, right?"

"I'm telling you, dope dealer. He'll be in jail in a few months."

"Thomas, come on?"

"All right, none of my business," he says, holding his hands up in the air.

*

"Well, with some dreams and myths, religious notions help us to know, and I quote here, "Dream is real." In other words, your real self will be revealed to you based on choices. Thank You."

Much applause. The hostess comes up and shakes Dr. Yates' hand, turns sideways, gestures to him, and the gathered applaud louder.

"We want to thank Dr. Yates for another stirring lecture."

The doctor takes a bow and walks to his seat on the front row.

"Wow, another good one," she says. We'd like to thank you all for coming tonight. Our next lecture is November 13, and Dr. Vincent Brown will discuss, 'What If I Knew?' his most recent thesis on Mung's personal unconsciousness. Goodnight everyone. Be sure to join us."

Shirley and Thomas were enjoying these small lectures at Freda Johnson's home. Twelve was about the right number of people for food and these kinds of intellectual classes. They both were readers and were well versed in this lecture series, and it made for a good date night as they seemed to be getting more serious about becoming a couple.

Chapter Five

Larry picked up the paper again and felt the anger, 'Forget American Blacks?' He'd kept it in a file folder under some clothes in the gym bag he's had since getting sober. He drifted in thought, away from the anger, to how he felt competing against the New York basketball players when he was in basic training in Missouri back in '72. He'd always heard the best 'ball' players came from there, and here he was, from Atlanta, Georgia, head and shoulders with these guys, dribbling, shooting, passing, play making the way he had against Blue and the boys back home. It was second nature to him just like the drills and marches, handling his pack, or helping Davis, the white kid from South Georgia who couldn't keep up sometimes, and how he thanked Larry for his support. Or the way he handled himself when the white drill sergeant from Ohio said in a class one time, "Make that brass shiny as a black man's ass;" somehow the sergeant had overlooked the only black soldier in the room, or perhaps he didn't care. In any event Larry went up to him after class and got a private apology, instead of making a big deal out of it.

*

Whatever the redacted parts of the paper were about he would like to recover them. Larry and the boys had survived different kinds of hell, here, and in Vietnam, back in the day, and they had come home to good jobs with the airlines, or the car companies; some to the Post Office, or airplane builders. Now, so many years later, it was when he ran into one of his grow up playmates, like Ralph Palmer, who still had that quiet calm and sense of fellowship they portrayed when playing for the Simpson Street Rams football team 50 years ago, showing then skills to master the game. His trials as a black heroin addict, compared to the challenges of combat in Southeast Asia, though different, yet the street gun fights of those Friday nights in Wedgewood qualified him as a combat participant. Sure, a different kind of combat, different hand to hand, different strategies, motives, and yet, the same need to play the cards as dealt, the same intent, oddly, to be a good man trying to do good things, and continually having it corrupted by the necessities of getting along, leading the 'men' on a mission to save the high school's honor, thinking of a simple fight when the troops had guns, and then getting kicked out of school because he was recognized as the football star, Larry Fleming; the others merely anonymous bad actors cheating a moral cause. And yet, now, talking to Palmer, both standing tall, mature, good men still, not bitter, or angry, older black men still ready to serve, still leading by example.

*

"Sometimes it's just hard to talk to black folk. The ones of us who stayed good, went to school, fought off the bad influences, and graduated school can't relate on certain levels. Or we didn't get the slave mentality, or the 40 acres and a mule thing, we just got up each day and went about it. My mother and father didn't have a master's degree, but they showed me the work ethic/payoff route. You know mama dropped out of college to have my sister, and daddy never went, but they just kept on," Darlene was saying as they rode the scenic roads from Santa Fe headed to Taos. "And, it was not pretense, just like it's not now. Certain kids I couldn't relate to, and that was black or white. Now, like your buddy, Roderick, he's a fool. I know you love him like your brother, and his wife and kids are precious, and at work, no comparison. But that boy is a fool, the language he uses sometimes, so out of date the way he describes certain women, and people in general. I just can't stand to be around him. And I know he's not going to change. And y'all get together for the Super Bowl, and I know you got it this time, so I just get ready. It's okay."

"Thank you. I know, it's crazy. And you know he's all about black folks, but his language..."

"David and your other friends cleaned up their acts, why can't he?" she adds.

"Look, there's El Chimayo. "

"Good, I got to pee."

They spent about an hour on the church grounds soaking up the October light, the fresh air, and the feeling that a force was at work to protect them if they maintained a spiritual balance. They were not church people back home, but still felt the presence of their ancestors, here.

*

Premium Photo, the subsidiary for research at Weapons Eye Sync was in the final testing phase for its most up to date device, the 1027BH. It not only could identify weapons, but gave vital signs, and could separate intent from motive in .79 seconds. The skin color issue was still troublesome, and that's why today's series of tests were so important.

"I still can't believe there's such a big difference in moral valuation," Dr. Timothy Lowe was sharing with Dr. Howard. "We've trained them, the feds 'trained' them, what else?"

"Tim, they're just different, and you can't change that. Nature/ nurture, Science 101 remember?"

"Look, how many white people do you see looting a store during a riot? Asian, Islamic, European, South American? You see what I'm saying? And what does the data show, starting about 1958, American Blacks are just different, and if you don't factor that in we'll never get the edge," Dr. Howard continued.

"Is that still that slavery stuff you guys down here like to hold on to?" Doctor Lowe questions.

"They do, and that's 60% of the issue."

"How about mixed race, slave owner's kids?"

"See, that's why we can't have this discussion. They too are different," Dr. Howard maintains.

"And what about their kids on down the line?" Tim asks.

"See, this is where Southern man messed it up for all of us, they're still white."

"Okay, I get that; bring in the criminals."

"One by one?" Dr. Howard asks.

"Yes, Dr. Lowe responds."

Unannounced, Thomas Robinson was in the parking lot about to come in. He was on his phone to Bruce who had mentioned today's testing and invited the boss. About the time Dr. Howard opened the door to the holding area Mr. Robinson was pushing it open. Thomas spoke to the temps there and had a quizzed look on his face.

"Dr." he spoke.

"Mr. Robinson, glad you could join us," adjusting quickly. "Is Mr. Walker coming as well?"

"Yes, he's about five minutes away."

"Good. We were about to begin. It will take about that much time to get set."

"Mr. Robinson, good to see you again," spoke Dr. Lowe as he walks over to him.

"Dr. Lowe, my pleasure."

Dr. Lowe continues past Thomas to summon the first person to come into the lab.

Dr. Howard was a bit surprised by that action, as he'd offered to bring them in.

"Mr. Casey, Orlando Casey."

A tall, fair skinned man stands, smiles, and walks toward the doctor. "Doctor," he says immediately.

"Yes," Doctor Lowe answers nervously. "Come on in.

*

Orlando Casey, 43, 6'1", 210lbs, drug dealer from Detroit. High blood pressure, no other health issues, served 13 years locked up, eight in the penitentiary, five in the camp, has been at the halfway house three months. Crack and marijuana, 121 IQ. Midrange dealer, possible murder suspect, not proven. 10 kids by four women. High school education, business courses at Georgia Perimeter, still controls a real estate business. Has $800,000.00 cash being held by relatives. Cooperative.

"Mr. Casey, thanks for coming. Are they keeping you busy in the warehouse?"

"Yes sir, four hours a day."

"I'm Dr. Tim Lowe, this is Dr. Howard, and that's Mr. Thomas Robinson," he gestures all around. "Dr. Joyce Taylor will join us shortly. Have a seat."

They all sit in chairs arranged in a circle, with two empties for Joyce and Bruce. Dr. Lowe continues to review the file on Mr. Casey. Then he begins.

"Mr. Casey, have you had a chance to read over the handout?"

"Yes sir."

"Do you have any questions?"

"Not now. Sounds interesting."

"I have a couple to ask you before we begin the testing."

"That's fine."

They all adjust their seated positions, with Mr. Robinson crossing his legs tightly, Dr. Howard shifting as if he has some back issues, Mr. Casey sitting straight up, and Tim getting more comfortable with the clipboard in his hand, dropping his pen once, smiling nervously, looking around, then begins his questions.

"May I call you Orlando?" he asks.

"Yeah." Answered in a friendly way.

"Okay, is your mother white, and your father black?"

"Actually, she's what you call mixed. Her daddy was white, and her mother was black."

"And you agree to participate in the line of testing as outlined on the form we gave you?"

"Yeah, it's all right."

"Okay, there will be a series of scenarios presented, and you'll act naturally. You don't have to be right, just right on!"

The group laughs at this attempt at humor. A gentle knock is heard on the door to the lab and Bruce and Joyce enter.

"Hello everyone," Dr. Taylor speaks.

"Gentlemen," Mr. Walker says, and walks to Mr. Casey, who is standing, introduces himself and Dr. Taylor. Drs. Lowe and Howard, and Mr. Robinson, who are standing as well, shake hands with the new arrivals, then they all sit.

"Well, Mr. Casey, thanks for participating in our study," Dr. Taylor says, as she retrieves a pen from her padded folder.

"You're welcome ma'am," Orlando answers.

There was an awkward tension in the room as they all sat silently for a few seconds. Even though Tim was the head researcher, this segment was based on data provided by Dr. Taylor.

"Dr. Taylor." Dr. Lowe announces for her to begin.

"Excuse me," the boss speaks up. "Mr. Casey, could you give us a few moments. Why don't you go back to the warehouse, and we'll call you when we're ready?"

"Sure, no problem. I still get paid, right? I finished my shift there for the day, and I have to return to the half-way house in two hours, and I can't be late."

"We'll get you back on time, and you get paid for the extra time," Thomas says.

Orlando gets up, nods to the group, and walks out the door, almost slamming it.

After a moment Bruce asks, "What's up chief?"

"Are you kidding me, or was this to be a fail test?"

"How do you mean?" Dr. Lowe asks, as well as Dr. Taylor.

"That guy's almost white, and I was feeling like he had taken over the room. Can you test for that?"

"Well, actually this was to be a 'cold' test. 1027BH should catch all that," Dr. Howard spoke up.

"And Dr. Taylor, you're sure about his lineage?" Mr. Robinson asks, showing some concern about her proficiency. I thought you were going to start the final testing on darker skin subjects and mix the rest of the schema?" Thomas asks.

"We could have, but everything to this point has checked out," she says.

"Bruce?" he looks to his partner.

"I trust the test design elements. Of course, what we must know is how sophisticated it really is, the ORT chip I mean. Can it filter for what you're asking in what, .79 second time frame? That we'll find out soon," Bruce says. "I trust Dr. Taylor's nuanced approach."

"Okay. Have the gentleman return, and I'll watch," Thomas offers.

Dr. Howard nods to Dr. Taylor with a wry smile on his face.

*

"What up?" Orlando asks as he re-enters the lab.

"Excuse us?" Dr. Taylor responds.

"Did you go smoke something when you went out?" asks Dr. Lowe.

"Well I went and hit a little something, you know. Y'all didn't have it together so I thought it might be better for the test. It's all about the test, right?" he says.

"You may be on to something?" Thomas speaks up. "Let's you and I act out the first scenario; step over here."

Mr. Robinson guides him to a table on a side wall; the others look on in awe.

"All right, here you see a gun, a knife, and a bent hook, eight inches long. I want you to choose one, walk about 20 yards down to the back wall, and face the wall."

Mr. Casey follows direction. Thomas goes over to a cabinet, takes out the flip phone like device with the keyboard and three-inch diameter screen. He touches a button on the side for three seconds, and a light comes on the screen, with a series of symbols and numbers. After a few seconds, the screen clears but stays aglow.

"Now I want you to think like I just cussed your mama out, and called you a fag, and a punk."

Before Thomas could finish the rest of his fake tirade Orlando had turned and was running for him.

"You motherfucker kiss my ass!" he shouted as he got closer.

When Orlando was within 10 yards Thomas clicked the control button on the device, once then twice. Orlando kept coming towards him but stopped short of bumping into Mr. Robinson. Everyone was winded by the rush of energy, and Bruce requested all to sit after a few deep breaths if needed.

"Wow!" exclaimed Dr. Tim.

"You got that right!" seconded Dr. Matthew.

Dr. Taylor stood, with a look on her face that suggested a mother about to say, 'boys, boys cut that out!' Thomas had the widest smile on his face as he viewed the screen.

"Yes, yes, everyone, sit, please," Thomas says.

They all chose the same chairs they had before. After a few seconds Bruce speaks:

"Mr. Casey, thank you. How do you feel?" he asks.

"Good, that was fun. Thank y'all for giving me a chance."

"Do you have enough time to get back to half-way on time?' Bruce asks, genuinely concerned.

"The buses run on time over here, and it's not rush hour. I should be fine."

"How's the warehouse?" Bruce asks, stalling a bit, knowing that his colleagues are dying to get the results, especially the way Thomas is glued to the screen, still smiling.

"Thanks again to y'all. It's great, a great job, and Frank is the best."

"Okay, good. When do you come back?" Dr. Matthew Howard asks.

"Next Friday," he answers.

"Okay, see you then, bye," everyone says.

He gets up quickly and goes on his way.

"Man, oh man, oh man," Thomas exclaims and twirls around to show everyone the screen, knowing they couldn't see it clearly, so he begins to read the results.

"Weapon-8-inch hook; intent-murder; motive-high; blood pressure-increased; ability-true; skin type-mixed race; time-.77."

They all clap, laugh, jump up and high five each other, some tear up a bit.

"Gosh damn!" Dr. Lowe shouts.

"Yea, Yea!" Dr. Howard screams.

"Praise the Lord," Dr. Taylor shouts.

"Amen," Mr. Walker adds.

"Great job!" Mr. Robinson affirms.

Chapter Six

Larry had forgotten to turn on the dishwasher last night so when he got up at four he turned it on. He decided to go to the computer to look up information for their trip to Hawaii in two months. They both were excited, and Darlene reminded him of their first trip to Hawaii, when they first got together. It was near Diamond Head, the Camellia Hotel, just across from Kapiolani Park.

The room they chose was a spiritual, restful spot with right angles and a king-size bed. It was airy, and the left side window faced the dormant volcano, with the ocean view to the right. The other window gave another ocean view, straight away between two hotels. The sixth-floor height afforded a special experience the night of the full winds howling past the bending palms and whistling around the secured buildings. From the balcony, you could see those shiny, glass, tall hotels at the other end of Waikiki, but that didn't seem as intimate, nor as close to the beach and the city life here. There was a floral garden near, which you could walk through, and open pavilions where various day people lounged. Across, and through the streets people jogged in trunks or bikinis. He also discovered a twelve-step meeting held outside in the park each morning, and he could tell his clients about the twelve Coconut trees nearby.

It was when they drove up Kahala, traveling east that Larry truly fell in love with Honolulu. Those homes facing the aqua colored waters, as expensive as they looked, and that whole Waialae region was simply breath taking to him. They drove some parts of it each day and seemed to fall more in love with each other as time passed. Yet, it was the drive to Hanauma Bay Nature Preserve that sent him over the top, and getting there being greeted by those low, salt and pepper clouds, and the overcast lighting filtering through, made the tuff ring design more haunting and lovely. Of course, those black and white TV pictures could never represent this beauty, nor the color screens of later years growing up; no, he could not visualize being in this vast expanse of wonder so far away from the mainland.

*

"Have you interviewed Mr. Fleming yet?" questioned Mr. Moran.

"No, we haven't. We've observed him jogging through the neighborhood, but he's hard to pin down. Plus, he lives near Thomas Robinson and Bruce Walker, on the same street, six houses down, on the corner," the agents report.

"That is a problem. Do they know him?" he asks.

"Just neighborhood social seems like, the once a year meet and greet kind of thing, actually four months ago."

"Did they seem like friendly; I mean comfortable?" Jack asks.

"Not like that," the older agent responds. "I don't think they have a working relationship with him."

"Do you really believe he still has the paper after all these years?" the younger agent asks.

"His supervisor from that night says he was reading something before they signed off. It took a long time to find him, and his memory was fuzzy. And there was never any suspicion about him anyway. He didn't come across as a reader."

"When was that?"

"Eight months ago."

"How long ago since Mr. Jackson had the contract to clean the offices?"

"Twenty-seven years," Jack answers. "And only he and Larry worked our area. Okay, do this, it's time to squeeze him, especially since Bruce and Thomas have their company up and running."

"The end game again?" the younger agent asks, somewhat playfully.

"A, find out if he has the paper, B, if he's read it, C, did he tell anyone else about it? Two weeks?"

"Yes sir," they answer.

*

"It's a lot of good people out there," Darlene was saying to Alice. "Good people doing a lot of good all the time. Too bad the news shows can only give us 3% of it a day."

"Yeah, they'd go out of business if they tried to give us more, '18-year-old black youth cut white lady's yard; didn't try to rob her.' Or, 72-year-old white man didn't have black youth arrested for sagging jeans,' Alice offered.

They both give out a big laugh.

"Why is it so hard to have a decent discussion about race in this country on TV?" Darlene asked, getting up to get more coffee. "Need a hit?" she asked Alice.

"No thanks." Alice gets up and follows her into the kitchen and looks out the back bank of windows to the woods behind the house.

"And it shouldn't be hard, especially down here since we all grew up together one way or another. Slaves, owners, maids, yard men, executives, doctors; since the early 1800s we've been connected," Darlene proposed.

"True, but that color thing just can't be overcome, and no one can be honest about that," Alice offered. "I was in the grocery store the other day and the pretty, young cashier resembled my niece, facial structure, long hair, cute smile, gentle features, body size, and I remember thinking, "But she's not quite as pretty. And I know it was skin color because of some darker spots on her forehead. And I don't know if it's wrong or not? Did she seem just as smart? Yes. Was she courteous, and efficient? Yes. Did she seem mean or angry? No. So, I don't know; but it was curious."

"I don't know. One of my girlfriends asked if I had not met Larry would I have considered dating a white guy. And to me the question has always been, 'Would a white guy consider dating me?' Now why is that I've wondered?" Darlene posits, "And the whole black man, white man thing is terrible anyway. I'll ask you, generally, do white men feel black men are as smart as they are?"

"Okay, we're going there. Generally, no. I think there is some relevance to the whole family dispersal thing, and I think there is a race color hate thing there as well. Seems like some black men are afraid of each other. But I digress. The point I was trying to make is that the whole nurture thing was set back, and I'll guess here, a hundred years in the black community."

"Because of drugs?"

"No, going back. The migration thing in the 30s, and the war years. That's my take: no science," Alice humbly offers.

"You know, I'll go with that. Some of the lessons grandpa had to offer were never passed down. Young men had to grow up without a certain structure that was put in place in the 20s by my granddad, and of course, the other blacks born at the turn of the century. They didn't have the extended formal education, but they had the family and the work ethic. I don't think I could manage my sister coming to live with us, and my grandmother talked all the time about siblings and cousins coming to stay with them at times. I think something has been lost there," Darlene shares. "There are just so many layers to this conversation, it's hard to get people to sit long enough and stay with each other's true thoughts, and histories."

"That's a good point," Alice responds. "We got help from some family during a rough patch in the 50s, but I think what was different we were raised to be independent early, though resources were around. If we were going to eat we still had to learn where to hunt. We were given a weapon, and time in the field together, but the duty was ours after they completed theirs. Or maybe put more simply, we were given 'stuff,' and the black culture didn't have stuff to give, and thus the uneven balance. Most black men didn't have the same means to prove themselves. It was a different kind of jungle."

They both pause, eye each other, hug, and cry for a time.

Chapter Seven

Wallace Henson had been drinking all day. When Linda arrived, he was in withdrawals. She had a key to his house and let herself in, only to see him walking around hallucinating, talking to the walls, looking under the bed, crying out for his mother, and trotting around the large living room at times. She was able to calm him by whispering his name, seductively. He came to her.

His face was red, his hands clammy, and as they hugged she could feel him vibrating.

"Wallace, Wallace dear, let me sit you down?"

"Okay, okay. What did you do with the little men?" he asked her, words slurred. "Are they still under the bed? Let's go see?" he blurted out.

She held his hand, and they walked to the bedroom where he promptly kneeled down and pulled back the dust ruffle, and announced, "They're still there! Look!"

Linda Adams bent down, pulled a portion of the covers back and agreed, "I see them!"

"Okay, good, just leave them alone and they'll go home soon," he announced.

Linda Adams, 42, RN, had known Wallace for six years. She viewed him as a father figure when they first met because he helped her out of a financial jam and didn't ask for the money back. It was $6,000.00, no strings attached, and even though they've made love on several occasions, they were not lovers; and she was not his 'daughter'.

"Wallace dear, when was your last drink, and sit here so I can take your vitals?" She guided him to a comfortable, yet low set Queen Anne styled chair.

"I'm okay," he grumbled. "I had two fingers about three hours ago."

When he was seated, and somewhat focused she wrapped the cuff around his left arm, bare since he only had on shorts and a white tee shirt. She grabbed a thermometer, put it between his lips, gently getting it under the tongue, and inflated the mini pressure machine. After a few moments, as was custom with him she read off the numbers.

"99.2, 185/100. A mess," she said to him. "Where's the booze?"

"In the cabinet," he said. "And my pill to sleep?" he asks her.

"After you eat. Come on."

*

Hobe had solved the transmission and reception issue with a smaller data processor. Their transducer, one quarter the size of a postage stamp, placed on the bone behind the ear, gives the signal of one impulse to shoot when activated. Its processing speed is .76 seconds.

"So, here we are, June 10, 2009, and the Pentagon people come tomorrow. Are all the results in?"

Jack Moran's boss, Shelley Hunter, PhD, was asking the research team.

"We're ready," Steven Foster, Jack's new assistant beamed. "We should impress them!"

"How about WES, where are they in the presentation line-up?" she asked.

"They're a week after us, and our information is that they are slower," Jack answered.

"Okay, good. What time?" she asked."

"The suits come at 6a and the brass at 6:30a," Steven responds.

"Where do we meet?" she asked.

"Performance lab. You should greet them up front, and escort them here to my office in case they want to talk informally first, allow them to get to know you better. I know them already. Steven will be here at 5:45a. A tray of bagels, pastries, coffee, juice, and some fruit will be in place," Jack reports.

"Do I bow down, give them a blow job, or what?" she asks with a laugh.

"No, these are the career people," Jack answers. "What they value is efficiency. Will this product help the soldier get the job done is all they want to know?"

"Good, my knees are hurting these days anyway."

They all have a good laugh.

"When you finish with the Colonels, bring them all downstairs; take the elevator."

"Will do," she says.

*

"The activators are responding perfectly, the sensors are fine, the semiconductors are great, so where's the problem?" Dr. Lowe was asking Bruce Walker.

"Data screens are great, and the assessment range is fuller, but these guys aren't really Muslim. They convert, ha, ha, in prison, and then go back to their old ways. Is this test going to help our Middle Eastern push?" Bruce asks.

"Well, we're just trying it. Dr. Taylor ordered it, so, we'll see."

"Okay. So, who do we have?" Bruce asks.

"Let me see here," Dr. Lowe says, "Okay, Jarri Ismail Johnson."

Bruce bursts out laughing. "See, that's what I'm talking about. C'mon man." Bruce continues to laugh, out of control laughing and coughing, then finally asking, "Why couldn't we get a real Muslim?"

"The one we had was sent back to prison on a violation. Something about denying him his religious freedom. Then he made some threats and predictions about what's going to happen to the infidels, and he wouldn't settle down. On, and on, and on," Tim says.

"Okay," he chuckles a bit more. "Just hold up, I'll talk to Dr. Taylor. This can't be good."

"Okay, we'll send him back home," Dr. Lowe says.

"What do mean, 'home;' he's not in half-way?" Bruce asks.

"No. He's been with us three months. He was in half-way for just two weeks. He didn't go through the program, so he didn't get any time off, a year they gave some of them," Doc responds.

"So, should we give it a try?"

"He's prepped and ready. We'll find out something," Tim replies.

"Okay. Is it all right if I stay, or would you rather have more leeway?"

"Just don't pull a Thomas, if I may?"

"You may. I get that."

*

Jarri Ismail Johnson, 44, served 18 years in the federal correction system. He went in when he was 26. He did three-years state time for distribution, and one-year state for assault with a deadly weapon. He was born and raised in Atlanta, Georgia, both parents Christian, good church people. He went to church with the family up until the age of 13, that's when he started selling drugs, and left home at 15. Dropped out of high school, four kids by Chakira Mosely, two in prison, the oldest in for life, murder.

"Doesn't stand a chance, does he?" Bruce commented.

"Actually, he's done well. Some infractions the first year, then he started studying Islam. Converted, studied the books, no other trouble in prison. Got his GED, a college degree in History, has written a few well received papers on his life as a Muslim in prison. We've not had one issue with him as a part time worker. As a matter of fact, half of his pay goes to savings. He lives with a sister who's a manager for Frankie's Deli on Tenth Street. Her husband is a cop. They have two kids. Kind of story book up to this point," Doctor Lowe reports.

"Okay," Bruce takes a deep breath, "Bring him in. I'll go to the observation area."

"Okay."

Dr. Lowe walks over, opens the door, and lets Mr. Johnson into the orientation room.

"Mr. Johnson, good to see you. I'm Dr. Lowe. Come in. How are things?"

"Good sir, all praise to Allah," he says.

"Have you studied the handout, your role in the scenario today?" Doc asks him.

Just then Drs. Taylor, Howard, and Morgan enter the room. With them is Terry Howard, an intern.

"Sorry we're late," Dr. Taylor says.

"As-Salaam- Alaikum," Mr. Johnson says.

They all look at him a bit surprised by the greeting, oddly.

"Yes," Dr. Howard speaks up. "Carry on."

Dr. Lowe starts the introductions:

"Hello everyone. This is Mr. Jarri Ismail Johnson who will be helping with our test today."

The others turn to him and nod.

"Mr. Johnson, this is Dr. Mathew Howard, Human Resources Director; actually, you have met, right?"

"Yes," Dr. Howard speaks up.

"This is Dr. Taylor," he opens his right hand towards her. "Dr. Andrew Morgan," he does the same, "And Terry Howard, doctoral candidate, interning with us."

After a brief pause and hand clasp, Dr. Lowe starts up again.

"I was just asking Mr. Johnson if he had read his material for today's proceedings."

"Yes, I have."

"Okay, let's all step into the lab and get set up."

They all turn, file through the opening, and get in position; Dr. Taylor in a captain's chair with a writing surface, Dr. Morgan with a yellow writing pad next to her, Dr. Morgan near the weapons table, and the intern at the other end of the 25-yard runway, as it were, with a timer in his hand, standing next to Mr. Johnson. Dr. Lowe is standing at the other end of the runway, arms down by his side, fitted with the 1027BH device, and the OTR chip behind his right ear. He had holstered a small handgun, .380 automatic; Mr. Johnson, as his instructions were, when he came into the lab, went to the weapons table, and chose the .357 magnum pistol. It had been checked and double locked so as not to fire.

As described, Mr. Johnson, a dark-skinned black man, was to start walking to his right, throwing his arms into the air, and start shouting, "Power to the people! Praise God. Yes, God. Yes, God." He was to spin around quickly, and shout, "All the people, all the time!" Then trot to his left, fall on the ground, remove the weapon from his inside coat pocket, stand up, then run towards Dr. Lowe, shouting, "All the People! All the Time!" When he was within 12 yards Dr. Lowe fired the test weapon, and Mr. Johnson fell to the ground, got up, and again ran towards the doc, who fired again when he was within five yards. Mr. Johnson fell again, arms sprawling, and his gun slid across the room.

Mr. Johnson lay there for a few seconds, as the room was silent. Then he looked up, and slowly started to rise. Gentle, slow applause began.

"Great job Mr. Johnson. Thank you very much. When do you come back to work for us?" Bruce asks.

"Monday. See y'all Monday. Praise God. Thank y'all."

Mr. Johnson dusts off his clothing, puts the .357 back on the weapons table, and exits the lab.

They all walk to where Dr. Lowe is standing; he has a perplexed look on his face.

"What's the reading?" Dr. Taylor asks him.

He'd taken the device out from its pouch hooked on his belt, at the hip, right side, and reviewed the results. As they gathered around he showed them:

Weapon—.357, criminal—yes, Intent—not to harm; he did not aim the weapon, mental health issue, device activated—impulse to fire was not sent, processing speed .76, operator error. Result—Dead civilian.

They all were taken aback, not of the science, but Dr. Lowe's "grave" error.

"I don't know what to say," Dr. Lowe sheepishly says.

"Why don't we take a break, then come back and do our review," Dr. Howards steps up.

They all nod in agreement.

Chapter Eight

As Larry got off the bus today he saw Rita sitting on her bench, rocking back and forth, with knit cap and wool coat on; it was about 40 degrees Fahrenheit this morning at 9:30. She did not acknowledge him, and he chose not to speak to her, though he felt guilty, as if he should. He did not have any clients scheduled today and came in just in case he had a walk in, or a referral to show up. He had brought the five-page paper with him to read. As he exited the stairwell and walked towards his office he saw two men standing by the door, one he recognized as missing group last week.

"Gentlemen," he greets them as he gets to the door and opens the office. "Come in, have a seat; I'll be with you shortly."

Larry goes to the four-draw filing cabinet next to a desk, opens the second drawer down, and places the paper in an unlabeled manila folder. He checks the fax machine, and phone message recorder, then returns to the reception area to speak to the men.

"Okay, who's first?' he asks.

Mr. Davis speaks up. "You may remember me, I'm Johnson Davis, and I came to a couple of classes about two months ago. I think I have eight left, and my probation officer said I need to finish, or go back to jail."

"Don't you want to go back to jail?" Larry asks.

"Hell no, why do you say that?" the young man responds.

"You haven't been here. Do you still have a job?"

"Yea, I'm still working."

"Well why haven't you been here?"

"Man, these classes are boring."

"So, your life's boring?"

"Nah, that's why I don't come here." He and Klinger chuckle.

"Well they will continue to be boring. So why are you here?"

"I don't want to go to jail."

"Jail's not boring, is it?"

"I thought you were a counselor; man you are tripping!" he exclaims.

"But I'm not bored. Go back to your probation officer, or somewhere 'exciting'".

Larry turns to Harry Klinger, who waits to see what Johnson is going to do.

"Mr. Klinger," Larry speaks.

"Ehhh, ehhh, let me think a minute," Mr. Klinger replies.

"How about me?" Mr. Davis interrupts.

"If you don't have anything to add to the group, don't come, like you've already done. We have fun here, talk shit, tell lies, and I get paid, and you get a letter. In the meantime, you might grow up a little, help someone else grow a little. If I correctly remember you and that meth were having a good time, so go back to that."

Davis sits back, a little perplexed at this exchange.

"Klinger?"

"May I be honest?"

"Sure."

"I don't like black people, so I didn't want to come back here after I saw you were black."

"I'm still black; why are you here?"

Klinger too sat back in his chair. Johnson speaks up.

"Look man." As he speaks Larry stops him.

"You know what, let me give you the names of some other counselors who may help you get what you need."

"Wait, wait," Davis hurries to say. "I like you. You're crazy. Can I start over?"

"Sure. Back to the first class. And every week you've got to have a topic to discuss. And I'm going to drug test you three times, and they all need to be clean for you to complete the course. $35.00 a pop. You ready for that, Mr. Excitement?"

"I can do that," he says.

"So, when are you going to start, this week, or next year?" Larry says sarcastically.

"I'll, I'll start this week. When?"

"Thursday at six; not 6:05 or 6:20. Six. You need to be here early to sign in, we rock and roll at six. All right?"

"All right." Johnson gets up to walk out and Larry says, "You owe $30.00 for this session we just had."

"What session?" he asks in amazement.

"Group. Me, you, and your buddy here. He'll owe too if he comes back."

"When do I pay that?"

"Now."

He bucks but reaches into his front pants pocket and pulls out some twenties. "Can I pay you for the first group now too?"

"And the drug screen."

"So how much is that?"

"$125.00," Klinger answers. "That's bullshit."

"Nah, that's all right, I'll pay now." Johnson Davis counts off six twenties, then reaches into another pocket and peels a five off a nice 'pool room' knot. "Here you go. Do I get a receipt?"

"Sure, hold up." Larry reaches into a drawer in front of the table and gets a pen and the receipt book out. He writes it, tears the sheet away and hands it to him.

"Thank you," Mr. Davis says.

"Okay, see you Thursday," Larry commands.

"Yep," he responds.

After Davis leaves, Larry tosses the receipt book to the table and holds on to the pen.

"Okay, you've had time to think," he asserts to the young man sitting before him.

"Counselors are not supposed to act like that," Klinger charges. "You act like a criminal!"

"I am."

"I knew it; y'all all are."

"My grandmamma is not one, nor was my grandfather. Just me." Larry responds.

"Look."

"Naaah, you look. Just go. Don't come back."

"Man, you are not a counselor," Klinger says, getting angry. "You're supposed to help somebody."

Larry does not respond, just sits, and looks him in the eye. Klinger looks away.

"No, I'm coming back." He reaches into his pocket and gets out a fifty. "Here, take your thirty. Give me my twenty back, and I'll see you Thursday."

"And who are you going to help?" Larry asks him.

"Race relations," he smiles. "You are weird man, but in a good way. Did you ever do drugs?"

"You'll have to come back Thursday to find out."

*

Bruce and Thomas were out for a walk this morning. Summit Chase was such a comfortable place to live, quiet, clean, with the power and communication lines underground. There was a good mix of maple, pine, and oak trees, as well as Douglas firs in front or behind some houses. About a third had crepe myrtles of various colors, cut back now because it was mid - January. The roads were wide, and the sidewalks were adequate in width, though not as wide as the ones in Bruce's old neighborhood on the west side of town. The sun was bright, and the air was just cool enough for you to know it was still winter.

"Do you think we've gone overboard with the technology?" Thomas was asking. "Just because we can, we don't have to process that much data; skin color, motive, and weapon are enough. And I'm not as clear as I once was about the importance of skin color, especially as we move into the Middle East, and then Asia. But we do need to discern religious commitment, so many Muslims. Their intentions are like ours, though they can be more rigid and conservative about social issues as their histories dictate. Certain moral principles for living must be adhered to, so speed, accuracy, and commitment is what we need to know for them, and of course weapons of choice. It used to be that way for the blacks when I was a cop back in the seventies, but they've gotten sloppy now, with mixed messages about not only intent, but also practice; we can't judge what they've done in the past to get a present moment reality check; so many don't know what real work is, or sacrifice for a cause, except getting high, or stealing something. That must change the biology such that we won't be able to get enough readings down the road, and our processors will be useless."

"Maybe," Bruce spoke up, "But we still have a great product that's saving lives on both ends."

"True, but was that Tim's fault last week?"

"Yes."

"So, what do we do now?" Thomas asked, partly to Bruce, partly to the universe.

"Let's stay with weapon, potential for accuracy based on skin color, IQ, and our response time. If we do those we keep saving lives and making money. Let Hobe play with all that other stuff, we're just businessmen, not political activists," Bruce conveyed to him.

"How do you mean potential for accuracy?" Thomas asked.

"Here intent and motive have to merge. Is this someone trained and practiced, or some nickel and dime hustler out to get party money for the weekend?"

"Are you talking terrorist?" Thomas asks with a bit of fear about what his partner is presenting.

"Well what are we selling to the Europeans?" Bruce asks.

"Well, we'll know when we get there. We don't have any contacts yet, but that should be a huge market."

"What do you want me to tell our researchers for tomorrow's test," Bruce asks him.

"Let me think about it some more," Thomas responds. "As a matter of fact, ask them what they would do with the technology we have to date, how can it best be used?"

"That sounds reasonable. I don't think we've ever done that?" Bruce says.

"Yeah, ask them; we may have to change focus?" Thomas says rhetorically.

When Thomas gets home, Shirley greets him at the front door with a kiss on the left cheek, and news that his brother Ron called and wants to speak to him.

"Did he say it was urgent?" he questions.

"Not really, just that he wanted to catch up. But he did say he has something he wants to run past you."

"Okay, thanks. I'll call him later," he says as he goes into the study.

*

Bruce had the hair on his neck stand as he was about to open his front door. The two guys jogging past out on the sidewalk didn't seem like locals. He knew it was reconnaissance and turned slightly to his right and sensed that they did not change pace when he looked around, 'professionals,' he thought.

*

"I think I'll go out to the mall," Dr. Lowe says to his co-workers. "I need to clear my head for about an hour or two."

"Okay," Dr. Howard says, "Would you like some company?"

"I'll be okay," he answers.

As he's walking towards the door Dr. Taylor notices he still has the receptor behind his ear. Also, he is so distracted he forgets he has the automatic pistol in his pocket.

Driving up Ponce to Peachtree and turning north he questioned whether it was just simply racist of him to 'shoot' the suspect in the test, and did his own prejudice override science? Or was it a simple mistake? He decided to turn left at Tenth to head towards the Georgia Tech campus. Driving past some off-campus buildings, he notices the diversity of students walking about. Within two blocks the world was already represented. He decided to park, walk a bit himself, grab a slice of pizza and watch the human symphony of higher education being played out before him. He stepped into Gino's at Spring and Eighth, ordered a cheese slice with broccoli & sausage, took a table next to a window, sat, and stared outside, not particularly focused on one scene: The slender black male, with the small, gray, backpack didn't particularly catch his eye, nor the heavy-set Arab student with his Indian girlfriend walking by, then coming up the one step into the cafe. They were kids doing school, taking a break between classes, or heading off to a part time job in the area. He did notice the attractive, middle age black woman sitting with two white colleagues laughing and referring to some passage in a textbook. They had to be professors, software techs, or programmers perhaps, he thought.

When the cashier called for Tim to come get his order, Dr. Lowe noticed the Arab pull a large gun from his waist belt before announcing, 'All must die!,' and point towards the threesome seated before him. Tim felt the sensation from his sensor, pulled out his weapon, and fired two rounds into the young man who buckled, then crumpled to the floor, lifeless. Doc looked around, assessing a solitary actor, returned his weapon to his pocket, and looked at his device's screen. It read, Weapon-AK, intent-maximum harm, skill-proficient, response-appropriate, time-.76secs.

Dr. Lowe helped secure the scene, waited for campus and Atlanta police to respond, processed with them, then drove back to the lab. Later that day while reviewing the recent test results, and Dr. Lowe's unscripted field experience, the team got to view the video feed sent over by Gino's.

"How did that feel?" Dr. Taylor asks.

"Good for the science; not good for the human, one for two. Life taken; lives saved. The device worked again! This time in the real world, hoorah!" Dr. Lowe exclaimed. "Thanks to you all for the support, and hard work," he shared with the assembled staff. "Dr. Howard," he addressed, "We need to fill Mr. Robinson in on the particulars here. Should I call, or will you?"

"I'm sure he's heard by now. I'll call him, and you call Mr. Walker," Dr. Howard says.

The calls were made, and Mr. Robinson invited them all out for a breakfast meeting in the morning.

*

Driving to Aunt Mary's Breakfast House Thomas felt lost and a tinge of fear. The financial scene was changing, and the uncertainty had those not already under contract ill at ease. He felt WES would be fine because of the positive testing, and the political atmosphere was hopeful.

"This is Bernard Harris reporting from PIN News, People in Need Radio, 650 on your AM dial. Our show is brought to you by Henson Technologies where sensors make sense. We'll start off with a view from the side, politics, religion, and where to find a good hot dog! Today is March 2, 2012, and the financial world is tense, credit default swaps have been exposed, foreclosure rates are rising, and a bright, new star is in the sky, Eric Jackson, the conservatives' worst nightmare, the mixed-race black man who they thought was 20 years away is here now and looking more presidential as time moves on. Let's draw a profile:

He's slender, good looking, born and raised in the great state of South Carolina. He's a beer man, and smokes cigarettes, Harvard Law, married to Marilyn Sims, Spelman lady, two kids. He knows church, how to rebuild communities, voter registration, constitutional law, and basketball. Not a Baptist minister, but a Senator, not from the 'hood,' slow to respond, and very smart. Didn't flirt with woman at gym who tried to 'get' him. Did I say smart? The college kids love him, the boomers dream, grandma is just happy to understand his speech pattern. He looks like a king, he talks like a surgeon, whoever he is let's look.

All right, I'll take a few calls and see what you think about a different brother from the South. Jim are you there?"

*

It was back in the summer of 2005 that they last visited Shirley's father in Wisconsin, Thomas remembered for some reason. It was his 74th birthday, and a large contingent from Atlanta flew up for the occasion. He and Marian were in good health then, and they were enjoying being retired. They walked the fields of hay cut by their groundskeeper after breakfast, when the weather was agreeable. They both enjoyed reading, music, and limited amounts of cable TV.

Their farm property was purchased in 2000, the year Gary Hester felt he had earned enough money from work. It was only ten acres, and the Sullivan family were part of the deal. They tended the grounds, the hay field, and had a sweet cottage to live in. Their kids had grown up here, and moved away, Anita to Madison and school, Jerry to Toronto and a movie making career. Walter and Anne Sullivan were easy going church folk who enjoyed the land, and the potent marijuana they could grow here. Gary and Marian would join them for a few puffs occasionally, but it was not a popular form of entertainment for them. Walter and Anne mainly smoked when friends came up from the south, old business and college friends needing to relax by carrying a buzz for a few days in a safe and open space, before proceeding on their travels west, usually to the desert.

Gary had resisted treatment for a degenerating disc in his mid-back, and Marian had a few general aches and pains due to her work at the bulk mail postal center in Duluth, Georgia for 15 years. She worked part time, and only stopped because Doc just didn't feel like his wife should work away from the home.

Dr. Hester had always said he chose psychiatry because the money was fabulous, and during the sixties and seventies he really enjoyed the scope of practice afforded him at Alexander Memorial Hospital in Marietta, and then at Apple Place in Dunwoody. He went to work each day to have fun, and his diagnostic and treatment skills were valued by his peers. He didn't like the way managed care took over psychiatric medicine in the early nineties, but continued to do good work, kept 15 staff members employed, and prepared for the comfort they were enjoying in retirement.

It was quite sad and poignant when Walter Sullivan called Shirley with the news that her parents, Gary, and Marian, had been killed in a car accident driving back from visiting friends in Reedsburg, just 10 miles away from home. Apparently, a rather large deer had come into the road in front of a car ahead of them, and as it swerved to miss the animal, the deer jumped, turned, and came towards them, and Gary hit it full on at 70 miles an hour. They, and the animal died instantly from the impact. Even though Thomas had set the place and time for the staff breakfast meeting he decided, of course, to fly immediately with Shirley to plan, and tend to any estate business.

Chapter Nine

Bruce felt rushed driving to the breakfast meeting until Mary called; "Hey darling, this is just an 'I love you call!'" she said.

"Thanks, Hon. I needed that. I'm a little concerned about our meeting this morning."

"Just be honest like we talked about last night. They all respect your experience on these kinds of matters," she reminds him.

"Okay. It'll be a few hours. What's your day like again?" he asked.

"I'm having lunch with Shirley; she's been tearful lately thinking about her parents."

"That's good. Tell her I said hello; take care."

"Okay, see you later."

Hanging up his mobile phone Bruce thought of a trip they took to Arizona when they were just getting serious about the relationship, and how they both achieved a new level of personal growth:

They both enjoyed the wet moisture of last night's lovemaking the second day they were in Arizona. Mary cooed upon awakening next to her best friend and lover, feeling so special that she and Bruce found each other at his stage of life, still young enough to push forward with new pursuits, and old enough to value the experience. Having Bruce was such a comfort, a man she had dreamed about as a youth, even drawing a face then that resembles him now. Her newer art works proved how much fun she was having moving from watercolors to mild acrylics, and more of an abstract presentation of her visual referencing. 'Spring Rain,' her second attempt, stuck to the canvas perfectly with no bleeding of colors the way watercolors can if one is not seasoned.

He was snoring and rolled away from her, shifting his thick thighs, and full waist. She pushed him a bit, not to awaken, but just enough to arouse the subconscious reception of a connection. She realized how the past few years have systematically led to not only a life partner, but the ability to reach in and allow her creativity to burst forth in unfiltered composition, and representation. She acknowledges that her depression had lifted, that her mood was brighter and not as bumpy, that for three years now she had not taken any medication or felt the need to disavow the happier parts of her experiences, that she didn't have to stay low and fearful. Now, her confidence could be measured by the course of their later dating, when she wanted to believe that he would leave, realizing she was damaged and could not sustain the relationship. That her moments of tearful anxiety could be accepted by a powerful, competent guy who didn't have these kinds of challenges, how she gradually was able to come to a greater acceptance of herself as vulnerable to the toughness of it all, that when her father died, she could find or have come into her life another kind and true loving man.

*

Bruce had been to the Grand Canyon before and knew the magical moments the shadows over the rocks produced. How that great expanse of air, history, and composition stole any sense of value and ego driven belief could accomplish anything this wonderful. There was something spiritual about how the beauty gracefully overtook any sense of power, or uniqueness. That the universe was certainly greater than its creations, that it took all parts of the cosmology to not only produce this wonder, but also allow the creations to experience and produce more of the same when actions are allowed for only the best; a tree, a flower, the honey bees, man-woman, red, brown, crème, all colors, all abilities, or deficiencies, all the personal conceits, and homilies, songs, tenets, and rules that try to achieve the same order and balance displayed here, when a hawk flies over, drifting on a motionless sky, peaceful looking, wings spread far, open, utilizing every ounce of biology to be up there, exploring, being, then coming to sit on the garden's arbor, quietly, looking, still, then flying off magically because it can, and must.

*

Aunt Mary's Breakfast House was a good place to meet and eat. It was on the west side of town in an older, gritty, working-class neighborhood. Within half a mile there were used car lots, small auto repair shops, large retail, and hardware stores. A large grocer was at one end, and several fast-food choices were nearby. The restaurant was a sprawling remodel of three smaller buildings, each spacious, with tables for up to twelve people to sit comfortably. The walls all around were filled with pictures of famous guests from over the past 30 years: athletes, politicians, local and national, a former POTUS, and his wife, and various entertainment types. It made for colorful memories as you walked to your table.

They all arrived on time, and a private nook was made available for the eight of them, as Thomas had requested the controller and the sales chief to attend as well. After everyone was seated and the waitress took drink orders Thomas called the meeting to order.

"Good morning again everyone. I want to start off by thanking everyone for their great effort in pulling WES together. I think we are all home folks now but let me make introductions just in case, and maybe say a few words about each of you. Of course, Bruce Walker, Dr. Matthew Howard, HR, Training, Dr. Tim Lowe, Testing coordinator, Dr. Taylor, Genetics, Dr. Morgan, Psychology, Intern, Terry Howard, Controller, Jan Perkins, and Sales Coordinator, Gerald Allen. And I'm Thomas Robinson, Boss."

Everyone chuckles politely as the waitress, Tammy, brings over the drink orders, and asks if they are ready to order.

"Tammy," Thomas speaks up, "I think we'll do the buffet, and you can take any special requests; anybody?"

They all seem fine with the buffet style.

"Okay!" she says, "I'll be a-checking on ya."

She walks off, and Thomas begins, "As you're getting your breakfast I want you to think about IQ, yours, and what they mean generally."

Several quizzed looks as each begins to rise and head for the food service line. After a few minutes, they all return with adequate starter plates, and Tammy brings in a large bowl of grits, extra toast, biscuits, juices, a coffee pot, and a couple of small plates, and strategically places them around the table.

"I'll bring some more jelly. Anything else?" she asks.

"I think we're fine for now," Bruce speaks up.

When she's out of the room the door is closed so that they can have more privacy for the discussion.

"I'll start," Thomas says. "I think I first knew I was smart at the age of ten. I remember being conscious of retaining information and wanting to discuss it with my father. I remember certain math games he played with a professor friend, a Dr. Josephson, and the first-time dad asked me to join in. It was a thrill. Next, I remember the first poem I understood, and I thought I wanted to write something one day like that. Then, when I was 14 we built a pinball machine, and dad would ask, "What goes here, or why does this work?" And I had to know the answers, as well as physically assemble the parts. Again, what a joy! Bruce?"

"Merci. Language. I loved hearing the spoken word. My mother had some German heritage, and she spoke the language, and my father learned it, and so did I. I could feel my brain smile the more words I added, and then, around the age of seven I became curious about France, and thus their language. At the end of middle school, I was fluent in each language."

Dr. Howard spoke next.

"Why people acted the way they did! In my early years, I was raised around an aunt and uncle who argued all the time, then would laugh like the best of friends. He would question why she didn't do something, and she would get on to him for doing something. It was confusing to me, and I would become emotional and cry. As time went on I would read the books I could understand about depth psychology, perception, and motives. How do you get a date at sixteen with all that running through your head?"

Everyone gives a knowing and hearty laugh that lasts for twenty seconds, with some choking mid bite of something.

"I wanted to know why we looked different," Dr. Taylor speaks up. "My family protected me from a lot, so I had to get it from books, and I found my way to the double helix and all that jazz."

"Statistics! Baseball, football, numbers and how they fit to mean something," Tim Lowe shares.

"Me too. Numbers, equations, and math puzzles," Dr. Morgan shares.

"Terry?" Mr. Robinson nudges.

"All of the above, except we built an organ."

"Jan, Gerald, you'll have another task later," Thomas offers.

They both give the 'chopped liver' move, then laugh.

"Okay, the test results, Tim?"

Tim pushes from the table and stands, as if to give a lecture with charts.

"Thank you for the breakfast boss. And all, thanks for the work. I think the 1027BH is the finest tool to help law enforcement around the world make decisions about intervention. If the user can know the type weapon being carried, the intent, and the ability of a suspect to do harm within .76 seconds I think the advantage is on the side of the good guys. Further, yes, my personal prejudice did override the science as I feared for my life, even though it was a practice event. I'm sure though, with trained professionals the likelihood of that kind of error is miniscule, even though we do consider race as a variable to be considered. And no, I don't know if the perpetrator had been a white person whether I would have felt, and I repeat, felt, the same way? The mixed-race test also presented one contextual problem because the sensors, like humans, confuse intent and motive, yet it was clearer on motive in this case; you could trust the mixed-race assailant to act, but with the darker skin the social issues are less reliable and somewhat of a bluff. And I don't know why that is the case. Dr. Taylor, anything?" he asks her to join in the presentation and sits as she gets up.

"Thank you, Dr. Lowe, so very well presented. What we find in the case of extremist, or people raised with a certain level of assurance the readings are truer, as Tim outlined. Yet, when we offer the device in the Middle East the issue of religion will come up, not as much in Europe, and I'll address that later. We must be prepared to offer a unit of measurement to deal with dominance, where certain decisions have been taken away from a possible suspect; they will be operating on forced belief, not choice. In Europe, the issue of history will be most important where desire and accuracy will be foremost. Thank you."

She sits, and there is gentle applause from Bruce and Thomas, the others sat almost frozen in thought.

"Matthew?" Thomas asks.

"Nothing now; very good."

"Dr. Morgan, anything?"

"Yes, thank you. Mixed race black politicians have not fared as well as one race politicians have. Since Mr. Jackson has become president social issues have destabilized."

Bruce stands and takes this one.

"What we're looking at now is that some of our competitors are addressing that issue behind the scenes. And some of the discussion is quite vicious, I might add. We must stick close to the mission outlined for Weapons Eye Sync. Some issues must be looked at in a new way, criminality, intent, just as we've talked about, and some other skin color dynamics that were looked at years earlier by a leading chip maker have been discounted. And that leads us into the whole IQ issue, we don't know where the knowledge-based economy is really going. There may be more of this computer, or rather, cyber terrorism, with a distant kind of brutality. You may not be able to get up close in certain cases, but there will always be enough foot traffic to warrant the use of our products. Thomas?"

Thomas thanks Bruce, and looks over to his controller, "Jan?"

"I just count the money," She jests.

"Gerald?"

"I just make the money!" They all give a healthy laugh, and Mr. Robinson ends the meeting.

Chapter Ten

Within two days Wallace Henson was feeling better and was back on the phones. His major contact at the DOD wanted more information on the super unit Henson bragged about having, and when could they expect to have a demonstration. "Two weeks," he had replied.

Henson noticed, though he felt better, he was shakier today, and the sweats returned. He knew he would have to take a drink to finish his work this afternoon. He was having trouble opening an envelope from his friend Helmut Conover, the head of Daylight Security Systems, who was hoping to spend time with him in August at the World CEO conference in Amsterdam at the hotel Scoren. Wallace opened his daily schedule book, flipped to August, and didn't see an entry. He tried to jog his memory, and started to ask Jake, but couldn't coordinate his next action without a few fingers of gin. He opened the bottom desk drawer, picked out the half pint bottle, let it slip a little in his right hand, almost dropped it, juggled it, and firmly held it with both hands. He twisted the top off, drank half of the bottle, put the cap back on, and let the half empty bottle fall back into the drawer. He wanted to call Linda, or Larry, but not Jake, who he was grooming to take over running the business. He re-grabbed the bottle and drank the rest of it, satisfied now he could make some decisions. After a few moments, he thought of August 12th, "Two months away. I'll let Jake in on the DOD situation; it's time he learned."

"How about the surveillance on my families? Why did Thomas Robinson really start up that company, and how is it that Larry Fleming happens to live in the same neighborhood?" Mr. Jack Moran was asking his field agents.

"Sir, we're still not sure after four months. What we do know is that Weapons Eye Sync, and its patents were registered back in 1986 by Thomas Robinson before coming to Hobe. Talking to cops who worked with him back then say he was a good cop, no major issues, only some racial stuff that didn't cause any friction. He's a decent guy," the older agent replies. "The only curious thing is that his wife, Shirley, worked in the mail room for the department for six years; that's where they met, but, she had dated a black guy in college, and obviously Thomas doesn't know about that."

"Really?" Jack responds.

"Well, maybe nothing, just seems like he's a racist to me based on some of the feedback we got."

"Do you think they've been compromised at all, especially the Walker family? Bruce is the one with the friends in high places, and his cover cannot ever be exposed! And what about this Fleming guy, research still believes he has something of value? They think he casually took something when he worked here as a cleaning person. They think it's the 824 Paper," Mr. Moran stressed.

Both agents shift a bit in their seats.

"Does that make you uncomfortable gentleman?" Jack asked.

"Wait a minute," the younger agent shot back, "he's a big-time drug counselor, isn't he?"

"Now; he has a rough history before that; dope fiend for sixteen years, slippery. He's been straight some twenty-seven, twenty-eight years or so. That's the legend you know about. He was very bad back in the day, so don't underestimate his abilities, period," Jack let on. "We still can't figure out why he's living in Summit Chase though? Could be coincidence, could be part of a bigger scheme? Just be careful."

"Please ask my assistant to come in as you're leaving; thanks," Jack commands. "Steven where are we with the systems for the DOD?" he asks him as he walks into Jack's large and impressive office.

"Sir, all systems are ready for shipment. All tests have been completed, we've checked and double checked, the range is standard at fifty yards now for weapon, skin color, IQ, intent, ability, dominance, and family of origin, .72 seconds is the accepted norm now. Very little variance in over 85 tests," David proudly reports.

"And when do you fly to Germany?"

"Next week. I'll take 30 units with me and two trainers."

"Good. Keep me posted. How's your mother?" Jack asks him, catching him off-guard.

"Good, thanks for asking. She'll never be the same. Tom was her light! She was so proud when he got that Star, 'The General,' she would say. He was her favorite, and a good brother to me. He served well. Just a tragic accident. Thank you for asking sir."

Chapter Eleven

Larry could sense the two guys creeping up behind him. He could feel their youthful energy and excitement. He understood the cadence as their steps quickened and he heard the swishing of their nylon jogging suit jackets. He became agitated with the ratcheted sound of the slide being pulled back on a semi-automatic pistol then released. "Young junkies out to rob the dope man," he thought.

He quickly went to his left pants pocket, pulled out a set of 10 keys on a thick ring and violently swung around clockwise, hitting the non-gun holder above his left temple, twisting awkwardly to the ground. From there he kicked the other college-aged boy in the knee, who accidentally put two bullets through his partner's abdomen, then ran away, never to be discovered. Sterling Jenkins, son of a prominent doctor, cried out for help as his lifeblood gushed from his mid-section. Larry told him to lie still, but the boy clutched at his stomach, crying, 'Mama! Mama!' loudly and eerily then rolled from his back to his stomach, and tried to get up, but fell and passed out. Larry tried to flag down a passing car but two of them sped away. Then, breathing heavily, he went to the door of the nearest house and yelled, "Help! We need an ambulance! Help!" No one answered.

When he came back to the scene, with blood on his hands, pants, and shirt, a police cruiser with blue lights flashing had stopped near the boy, who lay holding his sides and whispering now, 'mama, mama.' The police officer got out of his car, looked suspiciously at Larry, called for an ambulance, and began to question him. Larry, out of breath, gasping and fearful, was glad he didn't have any dope on him. The officer spoke to the boy, reached, and grabbed the boy's wrist searching for a pulse, then spoke into his shoulder microphone again about a possible homicide, and asked, "if there was an ambulance on the way?" Larry turned slowly a few feet away and the officer barked, "Stay close by!" as the boy now whispered for his daddy and mama, then became still and quiet. There was a slow hissing last breath, then a jerk of his left leg, and he was gone. The officer looked Larry directly in the eyes and asked, "What happened here?"

The wail of the ambulance took over as they both looked down the street to where the carriage hurtled towards them. The paramedics jumped out, grabbed equipment, and worked on the boy for a few minutes, knowing almost immediately by the bloodied sidewalk that he'd already bled to death. They talked back and forth, called their superior, lay the now covered body on the transfer board, and slowly eased it into the back of the ambulance. Several more police cars arrived while Larry told his story. The officers searched for the other boy and the weapon. They questioned Larry further at the 9th Precinct and told him not to leave town while the investigation was ongoing. He was later cleared of any culpability, but Dr. Jenkins wouldn't let it rest and at one point threatened Larry's life. Time passed and nothing more was said. Larry quit selling dope, left the streets, and got clean and sober a year later.

*

Larry remembered this event well after reading the story to the group. He was a little shaken and gave them a few extra minutes for break. When they came back together the group wanted to process the story further, but Larry resisted.

"We have some questions about you!" Harry Klinger asserted. "Who are you in the story?" he questioned.

"I'm not in the story; it's not my story," Larry lied without the group believing him.

"You are full of shit!" Sarah claimed. "You need to tell us who you are. You always say, 'get honest,' be 'honest,' and you don't. Is that a counselor thing? Somebody told me you are a writer too. So, you need to tell us who are you?"

*

The sales team was making appointments, gathering consultants, and re-training the trainers, and shipping product. It was June 2009, and sales were at $90,000,000.00. Thomas and Bruce were very pleased with the workforce and handed out bonuses equal to a week's pay.

"Have we taken care of the Tucker Country Club?" Thomas asked Bruce during their morning briefing.

"Yes, we have. We were able to get a retired Army MP, a Steven Jones, one of the sales consultants to speak to them. He was dark enough and skilled enough and they were doubly impressed with our device. We can use him often," Bruce answered.

"That's fine, very fine. Would you rather go to the CEO conference in August, and I take care of the people in New Mexico?" Thomas Robinson asked Bruce.

"No, I'll take care of the brothers down there. Amsterdam is lovingly refreshing that time year, take Shirley with you and make a vacation out of it. Plus, I have someone in France I want you to meet. It'll be a great train ride, and you'll love his goat farm," Bruce offers.

"Is this Henri, the baker's son you've talked about in the past?" Thomas asks.

"Yes, you remember. He would probably want a few units for his movement. I can call ahead if you decide to visit him there."

"Of course. Anything pressing today?"

"Thailand. The Rice King wants seven hundred units. I'm sure that's for resale, but that's his business," Bruce informs Thomas.

"Chechnya?"

"Probably."

"Who are you sending?" Thomas asks him.

"Dr. Howard I think. He has a friend who chased some young girl there, moved in, bought a little 'meditation' garden, and studies Hindu I think."

"You're kidding?"

"No, he was a retired economics professor, met her on some dating service or something, fell in love, and there you go," said somewhat sarcastically by Bruce. "At any rate, Matthew has been to that part of the world and should be able to move around there."

"Okay, sounds good. What about San Francisco?"

"Done. Three hundred units."

"Honolulu?"

"Two hundred, and they're interested in the skin color, IQ piece."

"How far out are we there?"

"Tim says two weeks."

"Good. Anything else?"

"Have you met our neighbor Mr. Fleming?" Bruce asks.

"The black guy on the corner?" Thomas asks.

"Him," Bruce says.

"Yes, once. He was jogging one morning at the time I was rolling out the garbage cart, about a month ago. He stopped, introduced himself, seemed okay," Thomas says.

"I think he's someone we need to get to know. I'll tell you more about him later, I've got to close a few gaps first," Bruce lets on.

"Okay, let me know."

*

"Ya daddy was home when you left, ya right, ya mama was home when you left, your right, sound off, 1, 2, sound off, three, four, cadence count, 1,2,3,4, one two, three, four! Left, left, left, right, left. Left, left, left, right, left."

Chapter Twelve

"Let me explain it this way, my name is Larry, and I'm a dope fiend. We'll do this tonight, but the best you'll get from it is your own life story. I'm a symbol of all the characters. Yes, I'm a writer. Yes, I stole stuff, and I've made amends, I've cut off long standing relationships, and I did get a very large settlement from a movie studio," he began as the group returned from break. "Most of you here tonight will have a rough road ahead, not only because of drug and alcohol use, but because you started so early. Part of your brain is already fried, and you won't develop correctly emotionally. If you stop now you increase your chances for a better life. The rest will get through this and never look back. Some will have a choice, and some will have it made for them. Most of the people I used with are dead. Died early. I'll take three questions, and how we'll do this is I'm going out for five minutes, and the group will decide the questions. And after we're done the rest of your time here will be about you and the educational pieces I present to help you become a better person. Okay, I'll be right back."

Larry gets up from his chair and walks out. Gina takes over.

"Let's nail his ass," she says. "I got a question for him; I'm going to ask him if he wants a blow job, right here?"

"Gina, get off that. So, you hooked a cop, big deal. Do you have a real question or not?" Joan asks her.

"Forget it; I thought it would be funny."

"We've been there, done that," Tori responds. "How about, should marijuana be legalized?"

"Y'all are lame. How about his philosophy on global, racial politics?" Davis asks the group.

"Yeah, and how about the exact nature of a balanced life?" Doris Jones adds.

"Okay, and how about is drug treatment necessary and effective?" Johnny adds in.

Lester Ross speaks up. "Did I miss the alcohol at break? When did y'all get here? I've been coming to group with a bunch of losers, and suddenly I'm in existentialism 201."

"What's that?" Sarah asks.

"Forget it. He'll tell you in his answers I'm sure," he responds.

After a few more minutes of discussion they decide on some focused questions. Larry comes back.

"Okay, here are my answers. Yes, I had a lot of freaky sex when I was out there. Legal Pot, I don't know; I smoked a lot of it. Race, our president has been good for the world. Treatment works if you work it. Balance is some things are right, some things are wrong. And lastly, I loved alcohol and heroin, and crank. Do I want any more, no? No cigarettes either. I love my wife, and my life is good; I did a lot of wrong back in my day. I have old calluses on my soul that may never heal. I don't like counseling the way I used to like it. I'm glad the new counselors are getting more education, book education, my experiences don't work for your generation. Did I leave out anything?"

The group sits in silence for a few moments, then Larry asks if there are any other questions.

"Does this mean you're like us?" Johnny asks.

"Not really. You have your own experiences, and answers. That's why I keep saying talk about you. I lie sometimes because even the good of my life is difficult against the backdrop of my past; the drug years were very terrible and mainly because I don't remember much of it. Some of what I did is quite disgusting and can never be repaired. You all have a chance, because of your ages, to have a much better life than you can imagine now, before you make some of those same kinds of errors. The complexities of my experiences are overwhelming at times, and what I hear most of you say is that this is no big deal. Counseling is about providing some hope that if you believe your present is troublesome, and you may not know that answers can be found that are simple and have meaning, but only if you have a concept of appropriate meaning to the human condition, and thus your part in this experience. Abuse of drugs and alcohol, if not cleared away, will rob you of that fullness of mind and body.

*

Larry could sense he was being followed as he left the parking garage and turned east onto Ponce. He turned left onto Barrett, went up a hundred yards, and turned into a driveway, backed out, and headed back to Ponce. He turned right, and from the rear-view mirror he saw the red car do the same. He drove further west, turned onto Monroe, and drove past Grady Stadium, and turned left onto Tenth. The red car with the two guys in it stayed just far enough back that Larry went into survival mode. He turned up to 14th, then over to where the boy hustlers used to work over on Crescent, came back out Peachtree Street then back to Ponce and the area where he used to roam those midnights long ago, those nights lost, 'geeked' up from the coke, loose from the booze, and tripping from the pot. He parked on Juniper, quickly ran up 8th, back to Peachtree, and around again, and knocked the larger of the two men over. Larry screamed, pulled out his seven-inch blade, cut the fellow, then ran after the other man, tackled him, and beat on his back and shoulders. He got up, ran for the red car, Larry caught him, cut him, screamed again, then slowly walked to his car, home again, but just a visitor.

Chapter Thirteen

Wallace Henson decided he needed to see his doctor if he was going to the CEO conference in August. He couldn't stop drinking and he needed to protect his business, and his employees, and that would mean informing Jake about certain aspects of the business that Wallace had kept hidden as a one-man shop owner. He trusted Jake, and he would need to step up and help 'daddy.'

"Jake, come to my office at 3," the message said.

After Henson left the message he went to his car and drove to Dr. Richardson's office for his 2 o'clock appointment. He was shaky but felt he could make it. He passed the police car, not even thinking about a possible DUI. After signing in and sitting in the lobby, he was shocked when the doctor came out and informed him an ambulance was on the way, and he was going to Northside Hospital immediately. He did not protest the doctor's decision about this, Wallace Henson knew he was in trouble.

Passing out before the ambulance arrived and awakening the next morning he didn't know he'd had a heart attack. The EMS techs were able to stabilize him with only one hit of the defibrillator paddles and had to deal with his foul language the whole ride to the hospital. "Drunks in a blackout," one of the guys was overheard saying when he signed off the delivery ticket in the ER.

*

At breakfast, the next morning Larry asked Darlene if they could talk over an issue he was having.

"What's up Hon?" she somberly asked.

"I think I'm being followed," he says in a blunt way. "I was followed last night after group, and while out jogging last week I could feel eyes on me that were not the neighbors," he offers.

"That's scary. Any reason someone would be following you?" she calmly asks.

"I'm not sure yet. If it were a vetting for a good purpose those two guys would not have chased me last night."

"You mean in the car?"

"Well that, and on foot."

"Baby let me make a phone call and tell them to have April start the training. You do have an issue, don't you?"

"Yes."

Darlene goes to make the call; Larry gets up from the kitchen table and sits in the den area. He fidgets a bit, stands up, and looks out the windows into the woods searching for the truth.

"Okay, where were we?"

"It didn't last long. I took care of it. I don't know why, they were just there," he says.

"Okay. What can't you tell me?" she asks cautiously.

"I don't know if they died or not. I cut 'em, that's all I know."

"Is this where I stop asking?"

"Yes and no. I may have to ask around and share a few things with you from the old days. It was quick, instincts I guess."

"Okay," she says slowly. "What are you doing today?"

"There's a paper I need to get from the office. I'll go get it and we'll read it together this evening."

"What paper?" she asks with a little more excitement.

"Something I should have shredded a long time ago."

"Do you think everything was clean from last night?"

"I think so; old playgrounds and all."

Darlene was used to Larry's double life now; she just never knew how the two could merge then separate so quickly.

*

Henson walked out of the hospital after five days of medical attention. He was fully hydrated, vitals were stable, and he had a desire to stay off the booze. He had even read half of a book the social worker brought by one day, 'The Big Book' she called it. He called Jake, asked about the business, and said he'd be in his office day after tomorrow, but wanted him to come to his lake house this afternoon. Jake agreed and arrived in Ellijay at 4.

"Apples," the man had said after giving Jake the street name of the turn he had missed. "Sweet apples. Be sure to come back next month," he said.

Jake drove the half mile back up the road, turned right and was greeted with one of the most comfortable sights he'd seen in a long time, an overview of mountains, trees, and streams rushing past, "The Country," he thought.

Ellijay was about 60-miles northeast of Atlanta with just enough back roads and northeast Georgia mountain beauty to rinse away the scum of city streets. The air was fresher, and the calming aspects of old, wooden shacks made weak by lack of use as farmers didn't sell sitting by the roads much anymore. Everything was closer to home, or the newer warehouse structures, same prices, same friendliness, however.

Jake was getting used to the slower pace and different use of the brain down south, same function, less information. His 'Philly' brunch had to give way to 'breakfast.' He didn't miss much of home, having gone to GSU for both degrees and now living in Roswell, which mirrored his hometown of Randall, Pennsylvania. As he pulled into the 60-yard-long driveway he wasn't sure what to expect from a boss who had allowed him to grow as a young executive, and nurtured his progress, but who had some troubling issues. Wallace Henson was bright and thorough and had made business decisions based on his step by step by painstaking step process to ensure success. To see him struggle with the bottle was perplexing to a guy who had sober parents who led a sound and easy lifestyle. A guy from a neighborhood that was alive and wonderful, with several races and ethnic persuasions blended to form a world view based on accommodation, and spending time to get to know what principles were important, and how to practice them daily. Jake knew how to live with others.

Chapter 14

Shirley and Mary were becoming better friends as their husbands' business flourished. They were out for lunch at the Thai WA Noodle Shop on Grove Avenue in Downtown Roswell. It was a small, upscale restaurant that sat twenty comfortably. The small two-person tables were mixed wrought iron and beveled glass, and the three that sat four were repurposed wood from a closed factory from around the corner, circa 1923. They were given a large table, and were glad that their friend Helen, who lives nearby, may join them. They sat, settled, ordered tea and basil rolls, and looked about the charming courtyard outside their window, to Mary's left. A gray feral cat could be seen scurrying past and running into the furniture repair shop next door, run by Kevin Taylor's family the past 62 years, 'Good Work in Time' the sign on the side of the building read. Seeing this, Mary drifted off in thought to the last time she and Bruce were in Hawaii. She remembered the peace and gratitude she felt for experiencing the 'out there' of that position in the Pacific Ocean. Her artistic nature was soothed by the almost hands-off approach of the sky, and the sing to me nature of the waters. She relished her love for Bruce and his ability to come home and sit with her, stroke her hair, look her in the eyes and truly ask about her day. It was all so dreamy and ordered by the universe that they could live a life of leisure, and yet, not have to move to a bigger house, or a better neighborhood, only because they had simply worked well and now enjoy a serenity preached by the deacons, those gentle souls of service who show up, and guide the reverend when he falls short, who support the efforts of the choir members, and class room teachers, who shepherd the flock, and pray for all as they are free. Yet, something was disturbing about Bruce that she couldn't quite put a finger on.

"Mary, what would you like?" Shirley asked, not noticing that Mary had gone to a parallel universe where the 'wiggles' of creativity reside.

"Oh wow, thanks, yes, let's see?" she answered still a bit cloudy.

They both look over the menu and order noodle soup with pork. The server brought their tea and rolls about the time Helen arrived. She took a seat, ordered what they were having, and grabbed both of their hands.

"So good to see you both; thanks for coming out this way."

"Absolutely," Shirley offers.

"You look well," Mary says to her.

"You too," she responds. "The rich ladies I always knew you were!"

They all laugh and share toothy grins at the fun of it all.

"How are those boys doing?" Helen asks, looking more towards Shirley.

"Just fine," she answers, looking to Mary who nods in agreement. "And how about Davis, is he still working for the pros?"

"He is, and he's doing great. In and out of town a lot lately; those athletes look good in their uniforms on Sunday, but they're a headache during the week; in trouble all the time, especially those good-looking black ones!"

"Helen!" Shirley responds.

"Of course, not all of them; but enough," she gives. "Every once-in-a-while he has one, with their lawyers, over to the house for a conference. It's all I can do to stay calm! Did I just say that?" as she blushes big time.

They all laugh and give each other semi-high fives.

"Do we need to move on?" Mary says, laughing the hardest.

"Yes, we do, to divorce court!" Shirley says.

They share more fun laughter.

"Have either of you dated a black guy before?" Helen asks.

"Gosh no," Mary responds rather quickly.

Shirley looks away and says, "Once, in college. A nice young man for about a year. It was nice."

"Just nice?" Helen asks.

"Nice, not enough sparks. How about you?" Shirley directs to Helen.

"Almost. It was supposed to be a double date before I met Davis, you all know Patty Hurston, well, she was going to set me up with her brother's friend; anyway, I couldn't do it. I wanted to try, but I just couldn't do it," Helen says.

"Your dad?" Shirley asks.

"Oh yeah! No way," Helen says.

They look away, smile, chuckle at times, then Mary breaks the moment.

"Have you decided about Amsterdam?" Mary directs to Shirley.

"I think I will go; it'll be fun. I've never been there. Either of you?"

"Twice," Helen says. "Once after college with a guy, then with Davis a few years ago. Great, romantic. We took train rides through Germany as well. You must do the trains."

"Beautiful in the country. I studied painting in a small village near the Amstel River for a month before dad got so sick. Be sure to rent a car. Study up before you go. Thomas is good about those kinds of things, isn't he?" Mary asks.

"Yes. He wants it to be business-pleasure. He loves driving around in new places. He mentioned something about France as well to visit a friend of Bruce's. But he's not sure," Shirley shares.

"How long?" Helen asks.

"Eight days. Two for business, the rest for fun!"

"The weather should be nice and mild, highs 70F to lows 50F," Mary says. "But check so you'll know what to take."

"I will, thanks," Shirley responds.

Chapter Fifteen

As Larry drove into town he thought of Rita. He wondered whether he should try to engage her in conversation or continue to listen when she speaks. They had been classmates, and though they were not friends, she too was usually at the top of the class in achievements. He remembered she had a brother and a couple of sisters and didn't think growing up anybody in their family was thought of as 'not right.' Her behavior now suggested schizophrenia, but since he was not a doctor he couldn't make a diagnosis. It was only odd that she knew things about him, and what course he was supposed to take. The talk of 'new dream,' and all that was beyond Larry's usual political involvement, though he had submitted a few short stories that had obvious political motive about race relations from his past experiences, 'positive experiences,' he thought. And he had written that paper freshman year of college about Dr. King. He couldn't see entirely past the fact that his present and past life had a meaning that was not intended by him, from street addict to esteemed counselor, hoodlum to good husband, good citizenship award to twice jailed. He understood that the past 28 years had allowed him to clear up the wreckage of his past, and help a lot of people get better, but there were still old things to make right. The incidents of the past few months were a bit unsettling and last night certainly was unexpected. Yet he was grateful that his skills for preservation were still tight and that when trouble found him, he could perform. Perhaps this was about a destiny he couldn't avoid, a purpose beyond his ability to steer. An unintended meaning because he was black, a meaning this country just couldn't shake. He hoped Rita had some answers for him.

He thought to drive past the bus stop to see if she was there, then turned right to go into the parking garage. He went up to his office and upon opening the door he saw an envelope on the floor. He picked it up, walked to his desk, sat, and opened it.

"Come see me, Rita."

He felt a chill throughout his body after he read the note. It seemed that forces beyond his control were again guiding him to participate in some adventure, something that was supposed to happen. He knew he wanted to end the groups and concentrate on assessments and individual sessions only but thought maybe he had a responsibility to the young folks, even though working with them kept his past life too fresh. On some level he wanted to disown it but knew that all those years of rough living had forever shaped his now.

He walked down the two flights of steps, went out the front door, and looked up the street to see if Rita was at her post.

Part of him didn't want to believe what was happening, yet he was going to trust it because this was his home area, and for whatever reason Rita had become his mentor.

"Good morning Larry," she greeted him. "I was deep in thought when you came by the last time."

Larry gestured to ask if he could sit, and she shook her head no.

"You are not a black man; you are a world man. Your life is not your own. The paper has a new dream. Get some crayons to scrub the missing words, blue and yellow. I will be away for a while. New dream. Tell them about the new dream. Be careful. More men will come. You need to get the device. Get a device soon."

Larry walked away, quickly now, with a sense of urgency to read the paper again. He had promised Darlene he would read it with her but as soon as he thought that Rita was behind him; "Your wife should not see it; she is not from the streets; she can help you, but she should not see it. That would change you. You must not change."

*

"So, who is this guy?" Bruce was asking his chief security officer.

"We don't know yet. We know he's very good with his hands. His military service was standard for the most part, he was a company clerk.

However, he did have a temporary assignment for two weeks that was redacted from his records. We don't know what that was about."

"And last night?"

"He's very skilled. We could try again."

"Let it rest for a while," Bruce ordered.

*

Henson was walking on a bridge over the canal yakking it up with Jake, and a military man in full attire. When Thomas saw them, he became excited thinking that either Henson already had a military tie in, or was working an angle here.

"Shall we go in?" Shirley asked, pulling Thomas back to her world. It was time to get food and relax.

"Of course, sorry for that," he says, still watching the direction of travel for the three men. Fortunately for Thomas they were headed for the same restaurant, and this would give him a chance to size up the relationship and arrange an introduction within the next two days.

Without Thomas knowing, Henson recognized him as the founder of WES, and was wanting to meet him to discuss business. They did trade eye contact and a nod that was part of the whole 'dance' of these conferences. Earlier, Thomas had met with Bruce's friend, the Frenchman, Henri, who was here on another business matter. He was able to share with Thomas some of the subtle word and gesture moves on this kind of world stage. Thomas didn't want to make any false moves, so the tutorial was helpful.

The next morning Shirley wanted to visit museums, and Thomas decided to go to the opening seminar. They had the breakfast buffet together and agreed to touch base at noon and see if he was free to have lunch together. If not, she would continue a tour of the area and take pictures for him to see later.

Chapter Sixteen

Larry decided to leave the paper in the cabinet, and he would pick up some crayons on the way home. He turned the radio on and heard the news report about two men being stabbed near Ponce last night about 10pm. The reporter said their wounds were not life threatening, and there were no suspects at this time. The victims were vague in their descriptions.

He thought about the paper he wrote in college about his hero at the time, Martin Luther King, Jr., and what changes he would make now, 38 years later. He thought that the paper would be the same, his hero is the same, only that now Rita had given him a challenge. King's dream was solid, and no need to change that or the true believers. His thoughts now were that history had allowed those believers and practitioners to live out the dream each day of their lives, before and after the great speech. Her charge was about the ones who didn't understand they had a part in developing the aspects of a new moral dream. The legacy she refers to are the immoral aspects that have become ingrained in a generation based on expediency, not moralism. They had come of age with a complexity not of their choosing, a complexity born of political correctness, of social dialogue with no genuine basis. He thought of the white friends' he's had over the years, and how they, for the most part, didn't like classical music, or opera either. They bonded with Larry because of his rough past, not his fondness for the fine arts. And that sore spot has remained to some extent because they are no longer around either, or this was not a racial decision on anyone's part; it was solely based on common interests, as before. Larry had shown that he was likable anywhere in the world when he sticks to the slightly above average lifestyle. It is only when he drifts higher to that lonely place and he feels most relevant that others have moved on because they still want the great athlete, or entertainer, never an equal or superior intellect. And yet, only a few are there and willing to show it. Too many are in prison, or locked down with the bottle or drugs, too many have conversations in places that aren't relevant to the place, too much street-speak, too much talk that ought to be done in the home because it is from the heart, misinformed at times, but always about the love. The new dream is simply about practicing the courage to be the best now, and somehow establish the new, prosperous, American Black culture. The new dream is about the blessed world community, without the weapons of daily destruction. It is about a love that only a sane, sober person can give.

*

The message to Jack Moran read:

1/10/2012

From: COL Steven Waller

Close Hobe immediately, it is no longer needed. You are to use only three staff to file, box, and crate all data and electronic communications. Ship that, and all equipment to St. Louis Storage Facility #5 NLT 1/24/2012. Use armored cars to transport. You are to report to Ft. Dix, NJ at 8:00am on 1/25/2012, to my office.

Jack was enraged when he read the memo. His outfit had done some ground-breaking work here since 1985, and he didn't want to go down without some acknowledgement. "No longer needed," he kept repeating to himself. He felt that their work on weapon recognition based on skin color and motive were more important now than ever before. Their device had it all, "IQ, intent, ability, and potential for dominance," he wondered aloud to no one. Jack was a career military man, and usually understood these kinds of abrupt changes, but this was his lab, his research, his data. Some very bad criminals were in prison now because of his stewardship of the project, and now, this? He knew he would move on, eventually, and let it go, but he still hadn't found that paper, the only copy; the original was in the safe. He would have to press harder on Mr. Fleming, the only person who could have it. 'I will not fail the mission,' Jack thought to himself.

*

Larry thought maybe he would go hit some golf balls before going home. He had his clubs and shoes in the back of the truck, the weather was nice, and he could use some time to not think.

As he pulled into Heritage Village, and drove past all brick two story houses, he was glad they didn't buy a home here when they were house hunting seven years ago. He loved the golf course, but the lots were small. The 2,500-sq. ft. of living space was great, and the unfinished basement was huge, but something never clicked about this being a home for them. Darlene was closer to giving it a try because her office is only four miles away, but like Larry, she didn't feel the 'home' thing.

*

Hitting off the first tee for a long par four, dog leg right, he placed the ball just off the fairway, left about 230 yards. His five-dollar driver from Rob's garage sale last year still worked well. He had 180 yards to the green and pulled out his four iron because he usually hit it straight, and this would need to be good. He took a few practice swings, lined up and caught it clean, with the ball bouncing twice onto the green leaving him an eight-foot birdie putt. He knew the green sloped quickly to the left, and he was thinking two balls out, maybe three, right for the aim, firm. He made it, hollered for joy, and drove on to the par three second hole.

After nine holes of practice he decided to stop and head home, first stopping to get the crayons to take with him back to the office on Thursday.

*

The 824 Paper in all its merits was very explosive thinking looking forward, especially based on the team's assessments of what the black, urban landscape would look like over the next 25 years. There was a belief that white America still wanted to be 'kids' and were not prepared to let the country mature. Even though space exploration was at a high level, and a lot of great things were happening in business, and global politics, and the sports world, there was a lot of negative change around, and Reagan's people had better develop a first-rate script, beyond nuclear tests in Nevada. A bad change was happening.

*

"Thanks for coming here tonight," Shirley was commenting to Thomas. "You seem more relaxed now."

"I feel relaxed, comfortable. We've had a great year in business, and we're both in great health, life is good at 62. You've been right, though, we do need to socialize a bit more. I was thinking of inviting our neighbors over, the Flemings down the street. Have Bruce and Mary come over as well."

"I think that's a fine idea. They seem nice enough. They wave, and smile. Have you ever had a conversation with either of them?" Shirley asks, as the server cleaned the remaining dishes from the table.

"Yes, briefly." "Thank you," Thomas interrupts, referring to the booklet with their bill in it that the Maître d has just brought over to them.

"How was everything?" he asks with a slight Spanish accent.

"Great, thank you. We'll tell our friends."

"Thank you."

He walks off, and Thomas can hear commotion coming from the entrance to the restaurant. He activates his sensor device, slowly reaches down to his leg holster, and removes his pistol. He holds it atop his lap, slides his chair away from the table a little, and sees the young gentleman storming past some guests waving an AK-47 rifle.

"Weapon, intent to harm, ability, high IQ," he had already read from the screen, and as the man aimed at the soldier with Wallace Henson, Thomas Robinson felt the sensation to act, and fired two rounds, killing the attacker. Everyone gasped, and gave space to where the man fell, pushing back in chairs, standing abruptly, and moving tables with glasses tumbling over spilling wine, and seltzers, and liquor. The scene quickly developed that surreal aspect and a heightened sense of survivor mode as people stood, looked at Thomas, looked at the assailant, and around at each other, as staff began the emergency calls to police and medical facilities, and found out that he had shot three persons just down the street before coming into the restaurant, killing one, near the hotel.

Chapter Seventeen

When Thomas arrived back in the states Bruce informed him that 6,000 units had been ordered since his 'performance' in the Netherlands. Also, Homeland Security had asked to sample the device. The training team will meet with them in New Mexico on the tenth of November. "What a year!" they both exclaimed.

After they discussed a few business matters, Thomas opened a letter that was from Henson Technologies.

"This Henson fellow, Henson Technologies," Thomas holds out the letter. "He wants to meet with us. He was at the conference, and we talked briefly. Do you know much about him?"

"Actually, I do," Bruce begins. "He's an accountant by training, he did audits for Hobe, and actually I met him first at Atlanta Scientific, bright, methodical. He did the usual numbers thing for a lot of years, taxes, buying and selling real estate, receivables, and then hit it big with a semi-conductor company, a once in a lifetime deal. He worked at it for several years, and through a subsidiary, Triple Line System, has made a mint. We've used some of his sensors in the 1027BH, especially intuition delineation. It bonds to our intent, and decision making CR2 sensor. It actually increased our recognition speed by .1 seconds."

"Well, I'll set up a dinner meeting, so we can see what he's like in the evenings," Thomas offers.

"That'd be great," Bruce responds. "I'll talk to Alice as well about the neighbors."

*

The area near the Buddhist Temple was hilly. Driving through a cemetery hardly seemed the ideal entrance to a spiritual retreat, yet it felt right. Alice would come out each morning, breathe in the fresh Hawaiian air, and walk around the pond. She enjoyed the beauty of the two black swans, and the multitude of Koi fish that moved through the water as if on a crowded dance floor. She prayed while she stood, watching their movements, seemingly rehearsed, like rush hour traffic in the middle of the week.

She had come to a decision about giving most of her money to charity, the 85 million dollars she won playing the lottery her one and only time. She was having plans drawn up to develop a foundation to intervene with black churches to promote education and civility. Standing there, stretching, breathing, drifting to here, present with her life now, she closed her eyes to visualize the aqua color of the ocean waters, she raised her arms, spreading them widely, accepting the island's fresh, stirring breeze.

When she returned home the phone rang just as she closed the front door, "Hello," she answers.

"Alice, this is Bruce Walker, one of your neighbors from Summit Chase, how are you?" he asks.

"Fine. You're who?"

"Bruce Walker, Mary's husband, Summit Chase back here in Tucker, Georgia."

"Oh yeah, Walkers, yeah, how are things in Tucker?"

"Fine, look, do you know much about the Fleming family, the black family on the corner that's been there for a number of years?" he asks straight-a-way.

"Good people, yeah, Larry and Darla, no Darlene. He's a counselor, and she works in placement or something. Yeah, there're good. They moved in after I did. Paid cash for the house. It felt good when I met with them," she gives.

"So, no gossip to speak of?" he asks.

"I don't think so. They're probably just like you. They've made it this far and they're quiet about it. I think he did retire not long ago but has an office downtown where he does something part time, you know, probably for taxes. Check with Bonnie Fuller next door to you, she may be able to help you. Better yet, why don't you and Ms. Mary have them over for a social?"

"You may be right. When are you coming back to Tucker?" he asks.

"I don't know. Take care. Goodbye," she says rather abruptly, put off by the imposition.

Bruce had not felt embarrassed in a long time, but he did now. That was a call he wished he had not made. "Well, it's done now," he thought.

Chapter Eighteen

Larry got to the office at 9am and was anxious to get the paper out. He had the blue and yellow crayons with him and was curious to see how this was going to work. There was still a part of him that wanted to shred it, unread, but he'd held on to it for so long. And how about Darlene, what would he tell her, either way. He went to the cabinet, pulled out the file with the papers in it, went into the reception area, and set it on the table. He sat, rolled the crayons out of the box, stared at the sheets for a moment and read:

Position Paper 824 (Classified)

"Race matters. The upcoming IQ tests will compare Middle Eastern and Asian subjects. We don't have to waste time on the American Blacks. That has been resolved. Yet, if there is a major financial crisis within 25 years..."

This is where the redaction starts, and Larry begins the up and across motion for each letter, blue stroke, yellow stroke, blue stroke, yellow stroke until he had completed the first page.

"and the right young black guy of mixed race has done some appropriate academic and community work, and is married with kids, he could be elected president, based on the disaffection of college aged white voters and older, white post-World War II voters. The old Negroes will come out from everywhere to vote, and a lot of first timers who may never vote again because they will be in prison or cracked out somewhere. Be prepared to act sometime in late 2008. Signed, Jack Moran. No one else is to see this!"

Larry started crying as he read. Rita's process worked, and the nature of the discourse here was disturbing. Larry wanted to call his mother, or granddaddy, some older black person and just say thanks, thanks for the chance to do my part, thanks for the effort you put in to bring me to this place: I will not fail this mission!

*

Larry read the other pages which contained statistics, and banal, recycled studies about IQ, slavery, 'The Southern Man,' workplace issues, and this new technology, the internet. He became a little disgusted, then released it. "I better call Darlene," he thought.

"Hey darling," he starts. "Busy?"

"Yes, extra training today, remedial work for you know who," she laments.

"Keep at it, it's necessary. Quickly, about that paper..."

"No worries, you know what to do. We'll talk this evening. Bye."

Larry felt relieved, then the phone rang.

"Oh, I forgot to mention, I've invited some neighbors over for brunch Saturday, about 10. The Walker and Robinson families up the street. I had a good talk with Shirley and ah, Mary, yes Mary last week and they seemed nice," Darlene offers.

"Fine by me," Larry responds.

"Okay, we'll talk, bye."

*

"Bruce did Mary tell you about a brunch we're invited to on Saturday?" Thomas asks before the start of the daily agenda meeting with the sales team.

"She did," he says with some animation.

"I couldn't believe it when Shirley told me about the conversation they had at the Market Fresh place last week, running into Darlene Fleming," Thomas says. "I guess smiles and waves do pay off eventually."

"I guess so," Bruce furthers the conversation. "Any thoughts?"

"I'm not looking for too much, just to be neighborly," Thomas answers.

"Sounds good."

Of course, Bruce did not let on how fortuitous this was for him and Jack Moran. His two guards had bungled their surveillance task, and now he would get a chance, up close and personal, but he didn't want to push too hard on a first date.

*

"Well that was fun!" Shirley said to Mary as they got into her car.

"I'm glad we finally met her. We've just smiled and waved for years. Is she a fountain of information or what?" Mary observes.

"And her inviting us over. I'm sure that's her Spelman training. Where did she say her husband went to college?" Shirley asks.

"I think she said GSU; but I don't think she said if he graduated or not?" Mary says.

"Oh, that's right, she said he left after three years to write poetry, and that he's pretty good. He's a drug counselor she says. Let's stop at the meat market before going home?" Shirley says.

"Sure," Mary responds.

Chapter Nineteen

"No, I did not," Wallace Henson answered as he was telling Jake about the response of Thomas Robinson to the attack in Amsterdam. "He was quick and sure, saved some lives, certainly General Leslie's; and with all the crime scene processing I was not able to talk with him further. At the opening class I introduced myself, and Helmut to him, as we were to go around and greet the other participants, but he seemed rushed, and I never had a chance again. We did exchange contact information, and I'll call him within a week or so."

"Their device is incredible," Jake adds.

"Because of our wafers," Wallace says. "What else do we need to discuss?"

"I left the most current organizational chart on your desk, as well as the revenue figures, and the research budget numbers. I reorganized some staff, and I do have a question about Linda Mitchell," Jake offers.

"She's fine. She's worth every penny. She's an employee, not my lover. No ethics problem there," Wallace takes over.

"I didn't want to be impertinent," Jake says.

"Jake, you have been nothing but discreet. And we can talk about the alcohol if you like. I'm sober 40 days now, I feel great. I go and see the doc next Tuesday."

"Shrink?" He asks.

"No, medical doctor. Heads okay. But thanks."

Jake lets it rest there but will document any strange behavior related to business.

*

Wallace left the Alpharetta office around two, drove down 400 to Lenox Rd., turned right onto Peachtree, and drove the mile and a half to take the left onto Rumson and his Country French style home in

Garden Hills. The 1938 house was adequate, and he'd done just enough remodeling for a comfortable, executive, 'man cave'. He could come and go with ease, get to the businesspeople he needed to see, entertain, and enjoy the prestige of the Buckhead address. The party strip was gone, the disco Kroger remodeled, and even the Gold Man Club was a church now. Wallace realized he had been operating in a blackout for years. His drinking had been terrible, and yet, no arrests, no bad sex stuff, no accidents, no robberies, and his businesses had all thrived. He felt his blessings and thanked the universe for a wonderful employee base. He thought he could feel a spiritual connection to it all, that even though his intellect had carried him a long way, some outside force had directed his choices, had allowed him to survive where others had fallen. He thought of Robert Tolliver, his college roommate, best man at his wedding, top lawyer with Southern Choices, how did he succumb to crack? Or Rick Jenkins, another attorney friend, busted with prostitutes? That was not supposed to happen. Both good men, decent. 'Lucky, Lucky, Lucky,' he repeats aloud as he gets into the shower.

After showering and eating a snack, he sat in the big chair and picked out a magazine to read, having checked the mail, and filed personal bills to be paid. The Law Enforcer Chronicler was a magazine that had stories of new tools, and how they were being used to save lives. There was an article in there written by Bruce Walker of Weapons Eye Sync, explaining the use of their next generation sensor device, the CR2. It was faster and transmitted more data than any other device available. It also had a range of 50 yards, which made it more useful to the military, and had an accuracy rate of 98.023.

"Wow," Henson reacted loudly, then thought, "And they're using our conductors; I've got to meet with those guys ASAP!"

*

Since basically being retired, Larry enjoyed his afternoon naps, and the way he could dream, the way he could fly to a distant world. His literary, creative side had returned and the smiles behind thoughts, and how they congealed to reveal an insight, a story, or a memory:

Something was wrong with Mr. Fred's left eye, or maybe he didn't have one. He kept the lid closed. He seemed kind all those years, the beret atop his head, and the resonance of his deep voice. He was a short, black man whose sickle cut the front and back yards at grand mama's house.

She always fed him afterwards, usually grits, eggs, and toast, with a large glass of water. He would sit humbly on the back porch, alone, singing sometimes with that deep, rich voice.

After eating he would come sit in the living room and flip through a few magazines, though I'm not sure whether he read them, or just enjoyed the pictures. She would join him at some point, and they would talk and laugh like friends do about this or that, always a cheerfulness between them.

I remember that one, yellow, late spring day when he came to visit, and Aunt Velma let him in. He sat, flipped through magazines for a short time, and asked about grandma. We had to tell him she had passed on last winter. He looked up, not at us, but outward, and after a time got up and walked out the screen door. I never saw Mr. Fred again.

*

He had grown fond of this last group and would announce tonight that he was going to be doing assessments and individual counseling only. He did not have the energy, or the desire to get the other necessary certifications to continue with the groups.

"So, this is our last group together. You all have done well. All the drug screens were negative. Why don't we go around the room and share any thoughts about the group experience and if you've learned anything? Sarah, you want to start?"

"No, but I will. I no longer smoke pot. I've learned to take it a day at a time, and I've enjoyed your classes."

"I just got community service, and I can keep my job," James shares.

"I have a boyfriend now, and I don't take sex lightly. I'm trying to grow up," says Gina.

"I'm just still here," Johnny says.

The others pass, or say very little, and Harry Klinger was the last one.

"Sir. I have begun to like other people. I don't like pot anymore. And I want to say thank you for being a good counselor."

As a group, they all clap and look around at each other, and Larry says their completion letters are on the table in the reception area.

*

Driving home Larry was thinking about Darlene, and how fortunate he feels to have a wife like her. He's glad she's enjoying her work and has supportive friends and co-workers. He hopes they will visit her friend Darla in the Spring and breathe in that fresh, restorative New Mexico air and openness again. He thinks he needs to tell her when he gets home how much he loves her and say thanks to her for creating such a wonderful home environment.

Chapter Twenty

Darlene and Larry made for a good-looking couple. They both were tall, with high, prominent cheek bones. She had what they called 'light' skin, meaning the color was not dark, and according to some circles an inherent 'better.' He was dark skinned in that walnut way very handsome black men can shine, and his features suggested smart, quick, and attractive. She was well groomed, wore tasteful, moderately priced clothes, good shoes, and turned heads whenever she was out somewhere, with Larry or not. He was more GQ light, sharp shoes, neat, pressed, clean shaved, and comfortable. They didn't have to impress, they just looked good.

Bruce and Mary were easy on the eyes, mid-range upper class looking with just enough pretense. They were the 100% cotton or Twill and Khakis types with button down, who could walk into a country club, or a football game with the same presence, assured, knowing, but a bit on edge. They both had clean skin, suggesting that life had not beat them up any, or placed too many demands on them, though you could tell Bruce may have had a few fights, or worked out well by his thick body. She was in good shape, and could lose a few pounds to turn heads, if she desired at her age.

Thomas and Shirley were the stars. They were not showy, necessarily, but you knew they spent money to have a slight edge on things. They were not going to lift a finger and risk getting dirty in what they wore. They both had achievements to be proud of, and second looks were expected, though not acknowledged. But otherwise, they were okay.

Neither of the three couples needed to compare bank accounts, they were all comfortable, relatively speaking, of course. Thomas and Bruce were very wealthy now, Darlene and Larry had invested well and made money from family estates that were liquidated over the past 15 years. And of course, few knew of the multi-million-dollar payment

Larry received from one of his short stories being made into a TV movie, without his permission.

"Hey, y'all come on in," Darlene greeted them at precisely 10am, as the Walker and Robinson teams had walked together.

"Hey, good to see you again," Shirley and Mary spoke, "thanks for having us over."

As they crossed the threshold no coats had to be taken as the weather was warm and nice for a mid-May morning. Larry walks up behind Darlene and speaks, "Hello, come on in." The troupe follows Larry to the living room, and introductions are made.

"Hon," Darlene starts, "this is Shirley and her husband Thomas. And this is Mary and her husband Bruce."

Good to meet you was spread around as the men shook hands, and the women nodded gently towards Larry and spoke his name. He then gestured for all to sit in their spacious, comfortable living room. Shirley and Thomas chose a sofa, with Darlene joining them, and Bruce and Mary chose single side seats that were firm and tastefully upholstered in a creamy beige color, with a white trim. The sofa was the same. Larry chose a chair that was a soft red that matched the Ottoman. The coffee table was two feet by four, solid oak stained darkly, with each board giving a unique tarnish. A fresh bouquet of flowers was atop in the middle, in a vase that could be called a 'vase,' (soft a), because it sure looked expensive. The rug, covering part of the foot and a half each square laminate tile flooring, was a standard, thick cotton floral with greens, reds, and some peach, that suggested an eye for quality and color blending. The cathedral ceilings, which all their houses had, made for a familiar setting, even though both Bruce and Thomas sat realizing this was the first time in their lives they had been in the home of a black family, and assessed that it could be one of their homes just as well. Shirley, of course, based on her relationship with Randy in college had been to his family's house several times, and Mary's family had a housekeeper for years and on occasion she had to take Ms. Ophelia home, and went into the small project apartment at least once, maybe twice, and met her family.

The kitchen as well was state of the art in a very practical way, with good appliances, granite counter tops from Namibia, a 44"x 36" island in the middle of the total space, 9" squares, white linoleum flooring, a sturdy, full breakfast table and chairs Darlene found waiting just for her at an antique flea market shop just outside the Perimeter two years ago, and a double pan stainless steel sink, with a single flow faucet. The walls here, and in the den, which flowed from the kitchen, and the living room had just enough pictures to soothe, and not overpower the senses. You wouldn't remember them once you left the house. Tasteful, pleasant, unassuming.

The lighting here in the kitchen, and dining room had eloquent three and five bell chandeliers that gave the impression of frozen poetry, as they say, captivating. The bedrooms were spacious, with the master being about 15'x20', and had a separate shower and Jacuzzi tub, with a full walk-in closet. After a tour of the garage and Larry's workshop, they all landed back in the kitchen to begin the rounds of coffee, juices, grits, salmon, eggs, breads, and pastries. The conversation was very safe and familiar to all with gentle references to race, business, religion, and politics.

Everyone seemed to have a good time, getting to finally meet, and offers were made to do it again soon. The guests left about 12:30, before Roderick showed up to speak to Larry.

*

"Oh, y'all hanging with the feds now?" Roderick announces while walking through the front door.

"What do you mean man, what's up?" Larry questions as he closes the front door, and they go into the kitchen.

"Larry, I know you did some spooky stuff when you were in the Army, and back in the day on the streets, but what's up with this?" he pronounces. "I'm sorry, hi Darlene, how are you?" he catches himself.

"Hey Rod, what's up?" she greets him.

"What the hell are you talking about?" Larry asks.

"Those dudes, especially the big one, rotten man. And the tall one, straight up cop. You remember when I was running that Maui weed with Herbert back in '89? Oh, that's right you had cleaned up by then. But anyway, those jokers are DEA. They took money, women, and the dope. That's why I didn't get no time. Herbert only got those two years because he had a state hold on him for possession; he could have walked too if he had told them about the other Larry, you know the hit man who drove that Coupe, shot that white boy down in the Bluff over that girl Charlene. You remember Larry from Detroit. Drove that 1971 Coupe de Ville, green with the white rag top. Them the ones that killed him," Roderick spoke, all animated and full of details. "So, what are they doing over here?" he asks.

"Rod, you my boy. Come on man, let's go out here to the workshop?" Larry offers.

"Did they go in there?" He asks.

"Yeah, you know, the house tour. Why?"

"I am not going in there to talk to you."

"What?"

"I'm just saying they might have dropped something in there."

"Come on man you're kidding me?"

"Let's take a ride, in my vehicle?"

"All right."

They turn back towards the kitchen and Darlene asks Roderick about the wife and kids.

"They all right. I was just in the neighborhood, and thought I'd drop by. What are we having for the Super Bowl next year?" he asks her.

"It's your turn to fix the meal. I'll set it up for y'all," she answers.

"All right, we'll talk about it," he says.

"Darling, we're going to the meat market; you want anything?" Larry asks her.

"I think we're good. Roderick, take care; say hello to the family for me," Darlene mentions.

"All right."

They ride off in Roderick's 1984 custom pick-up truck, and about a mile from Larry's house are pulled over by a police officer. As the officer walks towards the driver's side of the car, and within 10 yards of the occupants, he activates the 1027BH unit and views the screen. He gets to the window and asks Roderick for his driver's license and registration form, and looks over at Larry, and generally checks the inside of the vehicle. Roderick asks if there's a problem. The officer looks over the information given him, reads that it checks out, and hands the papers back to the driver.

"General driver safety checks in this area today. Thank you, you all have a good day," the officer says.

"What was that about?" they ask each other in unison and continue with their ride and conversation.

*

"Sir," the officer begins to his unit supervisor, "I had occasion to use the 1027BH unit a few minutes ago and had an anomaly. It gave an all clear on one person but could not discern any information on the other."

"How do you mean that?" The supervisor asks.

"Nothing. Did not send any data about weapon, intent, or ability, etc. Well actually it did register dark skin male, but nothing else."

"That's odd, I'll call the people at WES later to mention that. E-mail me a report."

"Will do sir."

"Thank you."

*

"All I'm saying is watch those dudes. Are you still doing the counseling thing?" Roderick asks Larry as they head back.

"Okay I will. And you're going to check with your boy at Ft. Benning?" Larry asks him.

"Yeah, soon."

"I've cut back, individual sessions, and assessments. No more groups." Larry answers the question.

"All right man stay down. We'll talk soon."

"All right my brother, see ya."

*

"Weapons Eye Sync, how may I direct your call?" the receptionist answers.

"Yes, Dr. Lowe please."

"One moment please."

"Hello, Tim Lowe," he answers.

"Yes, Doctor Lowe, my name is Jesse Thompson, unit super at precinct seven, APD, and I'm calling about the 1027BH unit we use."

"Yes, how may I help you?"

"Well, one of my officers informed me today that after using the unit for twelve stops he discovered three illegal weapons and prevented a potential robbery attempt."

"That's great."

"The reason I'm calling is that he says, and we have the printout, that on one person the unit was unable to give any information besides reading skin color."

"How do you mean?" the doc asks.

"Nothing about whether he had a weapon, any intent for harm, or his ability level. We got all that on the driver, but nothing on the passenger."

"And what you're saying is that it was something about the person, and not the unit?"

"Correct."

"Sir, could you send the unit, and your officer's report over today or tomorrow, and I'll get you a replacement unit. We'll probably need to inspect it thoroughly anyway," Dr. Lowe responds.

"I'll have a courier bring it over today," the officer says.

"Of course, thanks. We'll pay the courier, thanks."

Dr. Lowe pushes back in his chair, locks his hands behind his head, and drifts off into scientific supposition about this possible dilemma.

*

As he sat at his desk, he called Marie to see if she could come by for lunch. He could use her companionship today, away from the house.

"Sure darling, let me call mother and see if she can pick the little one from school if necessary," she says.

"Okay, call me back when you know; love you, bye," Jake says to her.

Jake was having second thoughts about working for Mr. Henson. He was glad his attorney put the jump clause into the new contract whereby he had 120 days to make sure this is what he wanted. He was enjoying the work and the opportunity to expand the business was exciting, especially due to the transmitters they've now developed, but Wallace's personal life was troubling on many levels. He was a drunk, a very smart, successful drunk, and Jake could foresee issues unfolding regarding how things would be done in the future. Wallace was a deal maker now and was getting used to dealing from the top and the bottom of the deck, whether you saw it or not, to make things happen. Jake felt he was cut from a separate kind of cloth yet did have some sense of the dark underbelly of high finance. He wanted to make sure he did what was best for all concerned, not just his benefactor.

*

Marie was slightly overweight, but otherwise in perfect health. She and Jake enjoyed playing tennis together and he still played basketball with some of his business peers occasionally. They both were evolving into their early forties' routine of demanding work and family-oriented activities as the kids were more active now away from the house. Marie handled the driving chores to schools, parties, sports, and piano lessons for Jessica, the oldest. And Jake was a good provider of money, so they acted like true partners respecting the roles they each had. They were the products of good parenting themselves, so they knew how to manage the daily household circus. They loved each other, and it was apparent by how they still held hands in public and looked into each other's eyes. Now that more money was around, they could enjoy the fullness of their lives, and still maintain the habit of prudent saving and future planning. They had a sparkle about them, more so together than separately. This was a union that was working, and the kids responded favorably.

"Mr. Austin, your wife is here," spoke his assistant.

"Okay, I'll be right out. Thanks."

Jake had ordered up a lunch special from Freddie's, a deli shop in the mall up the street. He wanted to surprise Marie with a 'thank you for being a good person celebration.' The flowers arrived about the same time Jake stepped into the lobby and he was able to see that honest expression of pure joy on her face. They hugged and kissed a bit as the assistant retrieved the flowers to put them in a vase. The lunch meal arrived about ten minutes later, just in time to cool the love birds who were about to "go all the way!" on the office worktable. The food was brought in, and the assistant knew that Mr. Austin would be unavailable for the next hour or so. The floor worked out just fine as cushions and clothes provided just enough comfort. Two people in love, comforting, reassuring, embracing, renewing those special vows without words, such an intoxicant, such a reward for giving of oneself.

As they ate and talked Jake was looking for the right opening to talk about his reservations without destroying the mood. This could lead to a big leap, or just a correction along the way.

"I do want to discuss one thing," Jake starts, taking a sip of water.

"Sure babe," she invites.

"Working here is great, but I do have some concerns about Mr. Henson. His drinking and how that could affect the company?" he begins. "Some of it is not my business because it's his personal choice, but I have to watch out for the business now."

"So true darling, and all these families," she says smiling and touching his chin. "Jake, we're here because of a lot of right decisions, and you know that. You're super responsible and good at this. I'm with you wherever, and I know you'll do what's best."

"Thank you darling, I needed to share this with you. I feel better and know if the time comes help is available."

"That's right, and you're never alone. You always seem to have a good sense of when to act and when to stay back. You'll make the right choices, Mr. President." She pauses a moment and looks out the window. "Okay, good, I'm going back to the other real world. Thank you so much for this pleasant surprise. I love you so much!"

"Same here, love you the best," he says.

They embrace, kiss a little more, and Marie heads for the door, looking back to see if his pants still have a bulge, then smiles, privately.

Chapter Twenty-One

Larry had completed his military assignment, and was headed to St. Peter's Basilica, and then to the Sistine Chapel. He had enjoyed the hillsides of Tuscany and into Florence where he was able to view the 'David' statue. He had just walked around it several times in awe at the majesty of an artwork so perfect, so huge, and so lifelike. How does one do this he kept asking himself?

Walking through that storied door, and experiencing the vastness of St. Peter's, Larry's eyes began to water as the feeling he developed was better than the rush of heroin. The evening rays of sun coming through the side windows high up, nor the ornate fixtures in the distance prepared him for the subtle elegance of the Pieta, even behind the new paneled glass protection. He stood there, motionless, a mother's embrace, and the adult Jesus, lifeless, draped across and against the bosom of all Christianity, the blood of humanity exposed by the vandalism of a deranged soul. He tore himself away, and viewed the paintings on the walls, and stopped at the statue of St. Peter, noticing the smoothness of the foot, touched, and rubbed, and honored by the masses. It was near six, and the march of the Cardinals would start, as people got in position for mass. Again, now, Larry had tears role off his face, his body shook with a rush of wonder, of total stillness as to moment, place, time, experience. He only knew a reverence, a respect for the artist, a respect for the honored experience of something beyond, and above the human condition of general woes about this and that, something that holds the races of man tentatively together, ever so string like, ever so film thin, yet, able to withstand the blows of power, misuse, and overly zealous defense of behaviors that are barbaric, dangerous, and yet, so much a part of why the species endures to this day. "Why, why have I needed drugs? Why have I needed those base desires multiplied to try and have what is freely given here, effortlessly, just for showing up, just for being willing to come, tired from a mission so dark, and deadly, so necessary, and yet, entrusted to a black man, not from the ghettoes, not from special education, entrusted to one who has to wear the burdens of a task not of his choosing. A task so powerful, and unknowable until that moment of execution, until that moment when the training and the skills match, that moment of life force entering beyond a meaning."

He stood, watched, prayed, and hoped that his life mattered, despite the disappointments, the errors, and plain old stuff that was not true to his being, yet necessary to a development for a cause. He thought, and felt all this, until he walked down the hallway, past those old world tapestries leading into the Chapel proper, the place where the creation is placed atop the world, a place where Larry, on the ground, had to look up for one hour to, what, understand, feel, experience, no, he just looked, because there are no words to describe the art of one man, one vision of the many visions of time immemorial, visions of hope, of pain, of wondering about the earth, being, stealing, giving, accepting, not knowing, knowing, yet, here, here, now.

Chapter Twenty-Two

One of the more useful selling points while the Mears project was underway had been the swimming pool and outdoor lounge area for exclusive use of the tenants. It had been carefully planned so that strict monitoring practices would always be in place. If a customer or client were brought to the area the lease holder would have to remain in the area with them.

Herman and Joseph Whitlock had stopped by the area on their way up to see Mr. Fleming for their 2 o'clock appointment.

"Good afternoon; come on in," Larry had greeted them. "I am Larry Fleming, good to see the both of you. Have a seat over here," he gestured to the sofa near the worktable. They sat, looked around the space, adjusted their comfort and shifted nervously. "So, what do we have today?" Larry asked.

Herman, the father, begins to talk.

"We have a couple of things. First, it's good to meet you. Sissy Lawson referred us to you and we're glad to be here."

Larry had a quizzical look on his face, then remarked, "Sissy, oh, over at 'To Be You Youth Center;' yes, good."

"That's right," Herman responds. "Anyway, my son and I are trying to work through some issues, and I'll speak for me and let him tell you his view of the situation. I'll be as factual and honest as I can be. This is pretty painful for me, us."

Larry notices the 17-year-old youngster is surprisingly calm and attentive to what his father is saying.

"My wife, his mother, of 20 years walked out of the marriage two months ago, drunk. She took off with some guy and we've only heard from her a few times." Mr. Whitlock begins to cry and pulls out a handkerchief from his right rear pants pocket, moist from prior use today. Joseph has a serious look on his face and twists his head from side to side in a gyrating fashion. "I've tried to find her, with no success so far. I don't know what to do. We talked to the police, and they say she's not missing because it was her choice, and if there's not been a threat to her overall safety there's nothing they can do, outside of posting the information I've given them. I guess she could be anywhere. I'm not a drinker, and she was not a drunk, I didn't think, but maybe I missed it working long hours, I don't know. I don't know; it's hard to live with." He begins to cry again and wipes his face with the cloth. "Maybe Joseph will talk now."

The young man has a shocked expression on his face as he was listening to his father and lost in his own thoughts.

"Joseph, anything now?" Larry gently asks him.

"No sir, not now." He looks away.

"Are you registered with 'To Be,' and in counseling with Mrs. Lawson?" Larry asks.

"Yes sir; twice, I've been twice."

"Are you going to continue?"

"Yes."

"Okay, good. Let's do this; Mr. Whitlock, if you want to continue I have an assessment form for you to take with you to fill out and bring back when you return, let's see, can you come back Tuesday, the 18th?"

"Yes sir I can."

"Joseph, I have a release of Information form for you to sign stating that you came today and talked to me, and I'll send that over to Mrs. Lawson, okay?"

"Sure, that's fine."

"Is there anything else?" Herman asks.

"There's my fee for today. Otherwise, here's my phone number. Call if you have any issues before Tuesday." He hands his card to Mr. Whitlock. "Joseph, Sissy is a fine lady, a good counselor. She should be able to help you through this," Larry says.

"How much for today?" Herman asks.

"Three hundred," Larry says.

"Is this for each time?" Mr. Whitlock asks.

"No. Individual sessions are $120.00. This was a family assessment fee."

"Okay."

"Call me if anything changes, or you just need to talk. It's a tough situation. Take it a day at a time."

"We will."

Larry hands Joseph the ROI form, and the assessment packet to Mr. Whitlock, who hands over a check to Larry.

"Thank you," they both say on the way out.

Mr. Whitlock forgot to mention the $600.00 missing from the family emergency jar that's kept in the pantry.

"So, what'd you think?" Thomas asked Bruce after the staff meeting.

"That was a great meeting. Good report by Tim," Bruce responds.

"Oh, I'm sorry, I meant Saturday, the Flemings?"

"Oh! That! Very well I thought. They seem to be a great couple. That was good. You?" Bruce asks.

"Not what I expected. I was expecting some loud talk and some poor me, some innuendoes about the white man not being fair to the brothers," Thomas shares.

"You're kidding me, right?" Bruce asks stunned by the references.

"That's what I see and hear when I'm out at the mall."

"Okay, back up."

"No, they are all just full of it. That was a good ruse, but I'm sure they returned to their normal behavior once we left," Thomas comments.

"Normal?"

"Yeah, talking about what white folks ought to do, that slang talk they use, they're not like us," Thomas further shares. "Anyway, that was enough for me."

"Meeting and talking to black folks on an even playing field?" Bruce asks him.

"Even? They will never have what we have, never. Oh yeah, they looked good, and the house was straight out of a catalogue, but come on, they're not like us. That was good acting. Period."

Bruce was not sure if he should share his surveillance information from the past and the present on Mr. Fleming.

"Okay. That's enough. How about today's testing?" Bruce asks him.

"See that's another thing, get them a straight out of the 'hood,' like they say, brother and sister to test. I don't mean family, if you can find one with the same mother and father, I mean a black man and woman with little everyday exposure to a better life, except what they see on TV," Thomas says. "I don't like 'em, and I never will."

Bruce withholds comment and walks out of the conference room, shaking his head from the inside.

*

The more Bruce thought about this conversation, and the request from Jack Moran he realized it was over, he really didn't have the zest for the intrigue any longer, and surely the racial attitude of his business partner couldn't be overlooked anymore; business products were one thing, and national security was another, but a total disregard of the human experience was something else. Money couldn't buy him freedom from that. Service meant something else as well. Sure, he and Thomas had done a lot of good work over the years, necessary, tough, hard work, and he could be proud of that. Going forward though, he wanted to maintain some sense of dignity and respect.

Chapter Twenty-Three

Larry decided to go and talk to Sylvester the shoeshine man over in the Fourth Ward to see if he could find out some information about Rita. He had developed this rather cryptic communication process with her, and he needed more assurance about what she's offering in the way of guidance.

The building was small, maybe 12' x 15', and it housed the shoeshine stand. It was set on a small parcel of land next to his house and had enough room for the bench that sat four, and an armchair for one. The stand was basic, a solid two feet high cabinet, four by four feet with the chair in the middle. It had the metal arm for one shoe at a time, and the client could rest the other foot next to it on a cushion. There were three drawers for his cloths, cans of wax, water bowls, towels, and various brushes.

Sylvester was a jovial, well sized man, 5'10", 210lbs. whose demeanor kept visitors in the mood of the day, quiet, reflective, or loud and talkative. There were a few regulars, old, retired guys who came and sat for varying lengths of time, to get a shine or not, and perhaps some alcohol was shared. Due to this location, and Sylvester's years shining shoes at the airport, men came from all walks of life, doctors, executives, hustlers, and blue-collar guys. Old friends and new, there was not a price list anywhere and people paid what they wanted; however, you would get a good shine and a few good moments of life.

When Larry arrived he recognized, obviously, former Mayor Richardson in the chair, and Fred Harper and Johnny Wilkes, sitting on the bench, drinking from small glasses. It was a loud day, and the laughs were full and inviting. Fred's daughter brought lunch for the gang and shook the mayor's hand and thanked him before she left. Larry greeted everyone and took a seat and joined in the conversation. After about forty minutes the mayor, Fred, and Johnny left, and Larry was able to mention his motive for being there today.

"Sylvester, do you remember Rita Owens, Lester's daughter?" he began gently.

"I do, sweet girl. She comes by sometimes and waves," he answers.

"Do you know much about her? She was a classmate of mine, but I don't remember much about her after grammar school."

"She was a little girl, and walked all over the neighborhood, everywhere. People would see her, and make sure she got home okay. But something happened one day, and the way I heard it she has not been the same since. We don't know what happened, and Lester looked around, and asked everybody, and he didn't find out anything, and she didn't say what happened. Of course people tried to say it was this or that, but nobody knows. Seems like she got married, or changed her name, or something. She goes by Rita Bishop now, and she says Rita Owens died. Nobody knows what she means, but she seems to know things that will happen, or she'll help people get something. We don't know, it's just strange. Anyway, when Lester died, and they started buying up property around the Mears place, it took some good people to save her house, some people Lester had worked for. Also, the developers had to set up an account for her, so she gets money to live on for the rest of her life. She sits over by the bus stop next to the building sometimes. Some folks say she owns a part of it, but I don't know about that. So why did you want to know?" he asks Larry.

"She's told me to do some things, and I get notes and packages from her that tell me what to do. I was just curious," Larry says.

"Well, you probably ought to do them, if not for her, but for other people if it will help somebody."

"All right my brother, thank you. I'll see you soon."

"All right."

They clasp hands and hug.

Chapter Twenty-Four

May 08, 1998, Training File: Jack Moran, Norris Henderson, Joe David. (Classified)

Jack Moran, head of the security detail, spotted him first this time.

"There he is!" burst forth for his excited recognition. "Same thing, small piece of paper in his hand, modern, black frame reading glasses hanging on his nose, jeans, t-shirt, this one saying something about a dream."

That look of distraction he always had was on his face today, yet, his easy scan of the immediate environment told of an attention, a focus, an awareness, an ability to move quickly with a directed response, if necessary. Jack thought him to be a thief, but Thomas and Bruce knew him to be much more. They had observed him for a year, coming into the store about this time of morning, alone, or with that woman some Sunday afternoons. They had decided he was from headquarters, and was sent with multiple agendas, but which, Bruce had offered, "we can't tell." Thomas went the racial discrimination route, Jack, employee performance. Bruce, if he speculated at all figured maintenance and cleanliness.

*

Leroy Fleming, Larry's brother, went to prison at 15, and got out at 33 years of age. He relocated to Arizona for a year, moved to Santa Fe, New Mexico for two years, then settled in to live on St. Simons Island back in South Georgia for twenty-three years. He has worked part time hours as a youth counselor at The Forest Treatment Center ever since. For the past two years he's handled special operations for his old friend Terry Barnes, the real estate developer. He married Celia Hutchinson, the artist of watercolor fame ten years ago, and they travel the world as needed to refresh their perspectives. She recently broke a big toe and has taken a break from painting.

*

Jack Moran was known as Stone Face. Ten years as a federal corrections officer taught him not to trust. Friendly people scared him, and anxiousness he read as a warning sign. He loved this line of work and knew his experience would help him survive. He knew if he were too open and animated, criminals would try to compromise that, especially the bank robbers he had caught. One, a west coast gang banger who was now used as a consultant. He had personally schooled Jack one afternoon during transport when they were locked in an elevator at FCI Talladega for an hour due to a mechanical failure.

"I always look to the corners of the ceilings first," he began. "I want to get a sense of space and time. Then, the height of the countertops, whether they would reduce response time by the tellers. I would smile when I entered, not looking at the women, only the men, usually seated at a desk, across the room. As soon as they spoke I would pounce," he shared.

"Since that day I don't smile at work," Jack offered to Bruce and Thomas.

*

Thomas was battling a gambling addiction. He had stopped for a year, started back small and irregular a month ago, and was now placing bets twice a day again, $200.00 each time. He was becoming sicker quicker and wanted to tell Shirley because he couldn't hide the money drain this time like before. He was not winning. Plus, he was not enjoying it at all. He wanted to confide in Bruce but couldn't own up to it yet.

Chapter Twenty-Five

"Come on in Dr. Lowe, what did you find out?" Thomas asks, as Tim comes into his office and takes a seat.

"Interesting. The unit worked great. What I did was walk around town, Midtown, Buckhead, and over in the darker sections on the Westside over by the stadium. Out of 50 activations I got 20 hits for weapons, and all the other measures remained true for skin color, IQ expectation, intent, and ability, relative to the area I was in," Dr. Lowe reports. "I did notice in Midtown, however, there were some disparities in racial make-up, that is the unit took extra time to coordinate for certain skin color variations. We may have to consult with the Germans on that."

"Why is that?" Thomas asks.

"Because of all the military presence the past 60 years they have more experience with cross pollination, so to speak," Tim comments.

"So, anything unusual?" Thomas asks.

"One thing. As I was entering the east wing of the building because I did some testing from Edgewood Avenue to here, I scanned this African American gentleman who came in after me. I got no reading on two tries. I got on the elevator with him and went to where he was going, and before he entered an office I scanned him again and got no reading."

"That's odd. What office?" Thomas questions.

"It was a counseling service, a Larry Fleming, NCAC, whatever that means."

"Was that Mr. Fleming you scanned?"

"I don't know. He was well dressed, you know, comfortable, neat, but no briefcase or anything. He probably was a client of theirs, I don't know?"

Thomas did not let on to what he was thinking.

*

"Bruce!" Thomas almost screamed into the phone, "who is that bastard?"

"Who do you mean, what's happened?" Bruce questions him.

"I'm coming to your office, I'll be right there," Thomas rushes to say.

"Our neighbor, the black guy, Fleming," Thomas says entering Bruce's office.

"You mean the guy you don't like, the actor?"

"We'll get back to that. I think Tim scanned him today and got no reading. And I think that's who the officer scanned when they contacted us about the unit. It works fine except on him," Thomas exclaims as he walks back and forth around Bruce's spacious office.

"Well you said he was an actor, and basically black folks don't matter, so what's the problem?" Bruce asks, with a bit of sarcasm.

"Help me out here man, who is that guy?"

Like the Walker family, the Brewers owned about 250 slaves in 1837. Georgia cotton and tobacco plants sold at premium prices, and their families ruled Truthland County, 80 miles west of Savannah. The soil was rich and deep in minerals, and money was being made. Rafer Brewer started out a timber man and wanted no part of the slave trade until his cousin, Julius Davis, loaned him two colored men to work the fields and he made 300 dollars that summer. He switched to cotton in 1825 and built his first house. He married Marie Thomas in '27, and Buford was born the following year.

Harlan Walker loved the land, and started rowing and selling tobacco in 1820. Cotton came his way due to a gambling debt, along with 15 slaves. He was the largest land owner by 1832 and ruled the town of Jesup. He and Rafer were decent men, but both of their sons were mean to the slaves, yet, fathered children by them, Buford six, and Grady Walker 11. They settled down by the ages of 23 and 25 respectively, and became good stewards of the land and their property. Both families passed on wealth and each succeeding generation became wealthier, and more powerful, however, due to a serious bacteria found in the soil, several offspring became sick, eight died, but three of the mixed ones survived. That was 1863 and the Walkers turned to politics, and stayed in the tobacco trade, moving most of their operation to Albany. The Brewers turned to the law profession and banking. They left the land and slavery just in time to maintain their power and influence.

The president's great, great grandmother, Josie, and Larry Fleming's great, great, Molly, were two of the kids that got sick and survived the bacteria, and developed an immunity to certain diseases, plus passed down a certain gene that would not allow for x-ray examination. Fortunately the families were stout, and didn't have much illness, or broken bones during the 20th century.

"Daylight Security, how may I direct your call?" The receptionist spoke.

"Helmut Conover please?" Bruce asked, speaking in the German language as well.

"Einen Moment bitte," she says.

"Helmut Conover, was ist los?"

"Das ist Bruce Walker with Weapons Eye Sync. Wie geht es dir?"

"Gut."

"Yes, Mr. Wallace Henson introduced you to my business partner, Thomas Robinson, at the CEO conference a few months ago, and we'd like to discuss some business possibilities with you," Bruce says.

"Yes, I've been waiting on your call. When can you come back over to this side of the world?" he asks. "I think we do need to talk. How about early December?"

"Yes, I'll call again, and we'll set the exact dates, okay?"

"Okay. Auf widersehen."

"Auf widersehen."

*

When Larry got to the office there was another envelope for him that had been slid under the door, again it was from Rita.

"This will be the last one. You're on your own from here. Good luck. Rita."

It read: 'Once you live a dream, and it is spent, it never returns; you hurt, but you never stop dreaming.'

Chapter Twenty-Six

Thomas and Bruce met on June 20, 2011, and decided to sell the company this year. They had met with banks, and insurers, and the lawyers were being consulted about necessary contracts. They felt good about what they had accomplished, and after talking it over with the wives they were ready to retire. They had worked together for 27 years in various capacities, and now wanted their true identities back. The government work had been tough, but a lot of bad people were in prison due to their efforts. To catch bad people, you can become bad, and they both knew they would probably need a little headwork at some point, especially Thomas, who already had returned to gambling as a source of relief. Plus, in his private moments, he thought more of his out-of-control racist views and knew that was part of the reason Bruce was wanting to leave the partnership. He was coming to believe that whatever perceived edge that gave him in human relations, most of his notions were just plain false. Sure, other cultural references were troublesome to him, but no one had asked him to wear a hoodie, or sag his pants. He never had to say, 'What's up G?,' or any other present-day expressions so many people use that were beyond the necessities of a 63-year-old man. Really, when he got honest with himself, he couldn't understand his culture, especially now to retire with more than adequate financial resources he wasn't sure what was appropriate for him to be involved in? This all seemed so, and he felt a sense of isolation.

Bruce, on the other hand, talked of the technological equipment Thomas had developed, and the products they had worked on together that would remain useful for years to come. It felt good to close this chapter of their lives, and start, basically, all over. They had been placed in the witness protection program in 1998 following the takedown of Grasevo and Murphy, the military trainers who moved pounds of heroin along with soldiers to combat. They continued in an undercover capacity until they left Hobe in 2008. He knew this separation was personal, and the money would soothe any discomfort about that. The business was a very good one, and the employees would be looked after with anything Bruce had to sign.

"Is there anything else we need to discuss today?" Thomas asked him.

"Probably not today; I'm tired," Bruce responded. "This will probably take about six months," he added.

"Well we've had a good run, and I have no issues with you," Thomas adds.

"Let's meet when we need to, and leave it at that," Bruce offers.

"Sounds good," Thomas agreed.

*

When Bruce opened the front door to let Thomas out of the house, six large, black, heavy-looking SUVs were heading down the street, quietly and in single file. They stopped in front of the Fleming residence and three men in full military gear jumped out and approached the house. After about twenty seconds, enough time for them to check the perimeter of the property, three others, dressed the same way, got out of the vehicle leading a professionally dressed female to the front door, which opened and closed quickly. Three more guards got out of another vehicle and the house was totally guarded and secured. Thomas walked to his house totally stunned by what he was seeing, and Bruce simply closed the door, picked up his phone, and called Leroy.

"She's there," he said, then hung up.

*

Bruce and Leroy had developed a curious relationship based on information Roderick's friend at Ft. Benning was able to uncover about Jack Moran. Jack was so angry about the missing 824 Paper he wanted

Bruce to arrange to have Larry killed, or he would expose the shenanigans he and Thomas pulled when they busted Leroy and his team of drug dealers back in the 90's. Of course Leroy's life had totally turned around, just like Larry's, and his wife, Celia, was a good friend of Mary's, Bruce's wife.

Leroy had told Bruce about the paper back in early 2008, and Bruce alerted the candidate's team about its implications for world instability if certain financial institutions were not protected from the oncoming train wrecks of financial mismanagement. Plus, the assassins' in waiting had been identified, and the inevitable candidate's people agreed to the change in leadership. 'He' must go on to win because the power shift was darker skinned now. Not everyone was on board, and the 'big dog' didn't like it at first, but he had more money to make, and he truly was a patriot. Personal family ambitions aside, the country had to be saved first.

*

Wallace Henson continued to enjoy sobriety, and enjoyed the meeting with Thomas Robinson, Helmut Conover, and Bruce Walker in Bad Kreuznach. Each brought business parts to the table, and agreements were reached to the benefit of all. Henson, by way of his Triple Line System subsidiary was developing an advanced transmitter that would boost the speed of the CR2 Unit WES had developed. Daylight Security's movement on accuracy and skin color recognition were helping every ones' sales numbers throughout the world. Henson would now formally name Jake Austin CEO of Henson Technologies, and he would maintain the President's title for Triple Line. The next few years could be grueling, and Wallace had gained a greater respect for Jake's business acumen and company loyalty.

Getting back to the States, and without a conscious decision, Wallace had a drink at an airport bar, and three hours later, after many more, Jake arrived in a limo to take him home, where Linda met them.

The next morning Henson 'escaped,' took a taxi to the airport, and got on a plane for San Francisco.

*

"Shirley! Shirley! Shirley!" Thomas exclaimed as he walked past the sofa and into the hallway. "Where are you?"

"In here," she says. "What's the excitement about?" she asks him.

"Come here, I need to show you something," he says, and ducks his head into the den, and waits for her to move.

"Okay, okay, what's the rush?"

"Cars, big cars at the Fleming's house, come see, armed guards, five I think, come here!" he shouts.

He pulls up the blinds to the window on the west side of the house and looks down the hill to the Fleming's house. Shirley walks up beside him.

"What do you think is going on?" she asks.

"I don't know but a well-dressed female went inside," he reports.

"Government you think?" she asks.

"You're damn right; has to be. I don't think its Wall Street or a drug cartel person," he says, feeling a little foolish now for the way he was acting over this.

"Well I'm sure we'll find out later," Shirley says, as she walks back to the middle bedroom that's used as a den.

"I really want to know what's going on down there," he says to himself.

He decides to call his old boss at Hobe, Jack Moran, who answers on the second ring.

"Hello."

"Hey Jack, Thomas, Thomas Robinson here; how are you these days?" he asks hurriedly.

"Not well. Rumors are starting that I may be shut down here at Hobe. I'm not sure. Nothing direct, but the pipeline stuff, you know what I mean?" he answers. "What's up?"

"Speaking of pipelines, I have something going on over here in my neighborhood that's odd. Several big SUVs have parked at a neighbor's house, with armed guards, and a woman gets out of one of the vehicles," Thomas reports.

"Black or White?" Jack asks.

"White I think, though a black couple live there," Thomas says.

"Do you know who they are?" Jack asks.

"A counselor and his wife, an HR person."

"Maybe it's her boss. Some of these company big shots have deep security now-a-days. I bet that's all it is. Do you know them well?"

"No I don't."

"Probably just some corporate stuff for show, or practice. How about a movie, they make a lot of movies here now, could be a movie?" Jack speculates.

"I don't think so. None of your people though?" Thomas asks.

"What's their names?"

"I really don't know, oh, Fleming, that's right, Fleming. I'll check with the local know it all tomorrow and see If they know anything."

"Okay, sounds good to me; but it's not my people," Jack says.

Thomas really wants to walk down there and get a closer look but doubts the guards would offer any information. He decides to keep looking for a while until ten minutes later Shirley tells him to give it a rest.

When he hangs up Jack begins to think that maybe it's too late, that the Chairwoman of the Oversight Committee will now have the paper, the one he signed from so long ago, the one that will end his career.

*

When Linda called and gave him the update Jake decided to handle it like a general employee matter whereby they took drunk and would be out a few days. If he hadn't heard from Wallace in a couple of days he'd do a search. Linda agreed.

Though Wallace was embarrassed and surprised that he got drunk, his creative juices were flowing, and he wanted to talk to some tech people out in the Valley about an idea he had for a long-range identification system that could tell retail shop operators if a customer intended to steal something. He knew a few engineers who worked out there, and he'd see if he could dialogue with any of them without giving away too much.

Meanwhile, Jake and Marie took the kids on a two-day outing to North Georgia to relax, and let the kids stretch out a little. Marie's brother, Jonathon, had some acreage with farm animals and such, and it would be good exposure for the kids to run around, interact with the chickens, and horses, goats, and cows, and maybe even get to see an eagle flying about the sky. They could breathe some fresh air and gain a little humility.

Chapter Twenty-Seven

Bruce and Mary were out for dinner at the Three V's restaurant on 8th Street. They were well dressed yet enjoyed the low-key atmosphere of the place. They could talk easily about recent events, especially the pending sale of WES. The past four months had been hectic, and the stress was evident as Bruce talked more about missteps he and Thomas made regarding some patents, and some sloppy legal work with Daylight Security that already cost the company $8,000,000.00 in fines to the German government. And dealing with Wallace Henson had been erratic as his financing had been approved, then delayed. They will know in late November if all is set for the closing on December 12, 2011.

"What are you having darling?'" Mary asks him.

"My standard pasta and meat sauce with broccoli crowns," he answered. "Have you decided?"

"Yes, Flounder, slightly blackened, with the vegetable medley and rice," she says.

"Sounds good, share?"

"Only if you beg."

They laugh and smile towards one another.

"Is there any way I can be helpful?" she asks him.

"Not now, but there are two investment dividends coming due soon from bonds I've held since Hobe. We can get you a new car, and roll them...I'm sorry, not now; relax, eat, love you," Bruce catches himself. "That's right, no money talk tonight. Gossip?" he asks in jest.

"A little," she responds with a twinkle in her eye. "I guess it's not really gossip, but I still can't believe how Thomas flipped out about the Senator's visit to our neighborhood. He still can't accept that black people are equal to anybody else, and that they can move in the same basic circles that we do or have. I mean, he's just lost it! He's plotting to have Mr. Fleming arrested. He wants to provoke him somehow, call the police, and make it a black and white thing, and ensure they take him to jail!"

"You're making this up, right?" he asks her, laughing.

"No. I'm telling you the truth; Thomas Robinson could use some counseling from the very man he wants to harm in some way. It's the gambling and Shirley says he was tested, and they found signs of early dementia. The neurologist ordered medication, but he won't take it."

"Do you think he's lost a lot of money?" he asks.

"Shirley doesn't think so, but she says it's 10, 15 hours a day sometimes; he's on the computer, he goes out to a gas station where they have tables set up to scratch off tickets. He buys a hundred at a time she says, five dollars each. She says he comes home with his jaw twitching like a cocaine addict, that's what the detective described to her, saying it's the same physical mechanism triggered by the gambling, at that level," Mary reports.

"Did the doctor say that?" he asks her. "Is he a cocaine addict too?"

"No, he doesn't do drugs, but he seems to be addicted to gambling, and the process is the same," she says.

"So she has a detective follow him?" Bruce quizzes.

"Sometimes," Mary answers.

"Wow! I don't see him much; we e-mail, and text, but the lawyers have all the papers. We've shut down the lab, and only a small staff is running the office for final shipments, and administration. That will stop Tuesday. The new owners wanted it that way, so they can have a fresh start," he reports to her.

"This is good," she says. "I may not share." She pauses to enjoy more of her meal. "So how do you feel about all of this?" she asks him.

"Not my business now. We are and will be very wealthy. I have no regrets. I've dealt above board since day one with Thomas and WES. If you mean going back further, of course there's much I can't talk about, but here we are, we've survived. I'm not looking over my shoulders, I'm at peace."

"I do have one thing?" she says.

"Ask."

"The DEA?"

"You know I love you with all my heart. Can I just say I was younger then and Thomas and I did a lot of good, hard work at Hobe, but we did some things not quite right. My exit from there, and the Norris Henderson persona was clean and final. All that's sealed up tight. I will never lie to you about any of that."

"Okay, I'm with you. Thanks. Now about that car..."

*

They found Thomas down near the Vine City Train Station with new clothes on, and acting from a bad Joe David front, certainly not worthy of his DEA persona. He had stopped in a men's store on MLK, Jr. Drive and bought an oversized gray hoodie, a pair of jeans four inches too long, and large by two sizes, some cool shades, and a baseball cap with the Braves 'A' on it that he turned to the side of his head. While standing on the South bound train platform he'd greet the young brothers with, "What's up my Nigger?" swinging his arms across his chest. Leroy and Bruce could hardly believe the video feed, but fortunately security had taken him to a safe zone before anything bad happened to him. They were going to intervene with Shirley, and have the police get him to The Avery Mental Health Hospital where a 1013 form would be signed by Dr. Leland. They would meet him there as part of the assessment and admission process.

*

Larry was glad he had given his brother Leroy a copy of the 824 paper years ago, even though he had not read it. Leroy didn't tell him what was in it back then either. Leroy was the operator, and if it came time to make some necessary moves because of it, he would and did. Even though Leroy was the younger brother he was more stable. Larry's need for art and poetry kept him at a distance sometimes from basic, everyday situations. Leroy knew Larry's darker secrets, and yet, had seen how he used those experiences to help those he counseled. Larry could go up and down the emotional scale and go deep and dark psychiatrically. He could laugh as well to clean or dirty jokes, though he preferred them clean. They both had sold drugs, but Larry had become the international addict. Fortunately, he survived using some of the best heroin in the world back in the early seventies. Once he cleaned up, and worked from the street up, people far and wide sought out his counsel. A young preacher's son, full of anger and prejudice towards junkies and prostitutes, came to see Larry who confronted him about his own marriage, and parenting style, and was able to watch the man cry and confess his 'sins' before becoming a preacher himself, who afterwards softened his message and now has a loyal following. Or the Aerospace engineer who in a heightened cocaine state probably killed somebody and needed to get honest about that with himself, and how Larry deftly avoided a legal problem for both by having the man write it down on paper, and then destroying the note. The man later got into recovery and built a successful business which employs hundreds during the summer. Or the young family whose father could not stop drinking, and the effort he put into talking with the man and his wife, checking on him often. It was a sad night when the woman came to tell Larry the man had died, and she just wanted to thank him for spending the time with her husband, who had voiced his appreciation to her. Or helping the Whitlock family recently bridge the pain of infidelity fueled by alcohol, helping a mother regain her dignity, and a father find graciousness, and humility. Also, helping a son find his own strength to move forward and attend college after therapy.

*

Larry never bragged about his work, as he adhered to the strictest code of ethics and professional behavior. But he was from the streets by choice and used his survival as a show of force to help others find their true voice. He was a counselor, not a drug and alcohol counselor, or alcohol and drug specialist, a counselor, who knew human strengths and weaknesses, who knew the power of a life force so special few could control or believe it, without turning to the trite, or the convenient.

The day the police questioned him outside the bank, they only saw a black man with a skull cap and muddied coat get out of a beat-up truck, walk towards the bank's front door, answer his mobile, and begin a full conversation, walking, no, pacing back and around the truck, standing at the back of it, going near the door of the bank, and turning back. They had no way of knowing, and he did not tell them, that a friend was distraught, and threatening suicide, and rather than tend to his banking business immediately, and call back, he chose to answer the phone and stay with his friend until he agreed to get help. Also, by looks, they had no way of knowing he was a multi-millionaire and that his casual attire was suited for the weather and a basement water leak he had just fixed for a neighbor. And surely, he did not look like someone about to deposit $50,000.00 to a money market account.

He even thanked them for being so diligent about their work, and understood why they had to check him out, discovering he was a veteran, all registrations were in order, and that he hadn't received a driving ticket in over twenty years.

*

Darlene had the benefit of stable role models and knew how to be a woman for her man, and she allowed him to be the man for her. She never asked some of the big questions about his past, and he never offered answers, so as not to frighten her. She knew his lies were protective and not to harm, and she could not absorb the depth of street life he had lived. When they met, he had solved that, but he understood he was forever shaped by his past, that certain behaviors were in his bloodstream. He understood the ambiguities of 'junkie man,' and a swift, true mission to rectify the murders of seven young black soldiers by officers having fun. He could pray that granddaddy watched over him, and that he needed grand-mama's call for limits as to who he should play with. He was a big boy, but she never saw how big he became. The whole thing with Rita was clearer now, it wasn't a speech, it wouldn't be a book, Larry had to witness for his special grace, away from the noise of TV land. The new dream was in him, and everyone else had the new dream of family pride, and achievements galore. Those daily tasks delivered simply, a step at a time, going up the ladder.

Chapter Twenty-Eight

Within 36 hours Wallace Henson had found two female engineers who signed the necessary non-disclosure forms, work for hire contracts, and proprietary use agreements, and then demonstrated the necessary electrical and mechanical knowledge to take the schematics he brought, design and develop a prototype that worked, and helped him to sober up. He paid them $6,000.00 each and left with a new product. He e-mailed Jake that he would be in the office Thursday, and for him to alert the lab about testing a potential new product for compatibility with their 641 transmitter and sensor device. The jumbo jet could not fly back to Georgia fast enough.

*

Larry was having a master class for poetry in his head today. "Is it trauma or drama?" he laughed to himself. Some of what he enjoyed about intellectual rambling was that he had gone where it led: museums here, San Fran, LA, Phoenix, Santa Fe, Memphis, and Rome. Or the pieces of music that would capture a mood, the Rachmaninoff 2nd piano concerto, Mahler's 6th, any number of the rock and roll greats from the 60s and 70s, R&B all night long. Ballet performances in 1974, or, The Iliad and The Odyssey, Hegel, Hardy, Baldwin, Christie, Tillich, all took turns expressing their views upon the state of Larry's life as a 64-year-old black man in America, which they were not making that distinction today. He was a 64-year-old man with the joys and heartaches of the living, the triumphs and failures, the washed-out plans, the serendipity. He was trying to balance it all as he walked about the Saturday Fresh Street Market in downtown Madison, Wisconsin, again, not many brown people, but yet, people going about the business of commerce, trade, friends stopping to give updates on the kids, or mama and them, intimate eyes watching, protecting, freeing up new space for new people, experiences, or thoughts, feet passing by stressed, comfortable, old, worn, used. The openness always changed him, roads, long, flat, going away to the smaller towns, large deer, fresher air, hay fields, cows, manure smells, farms, orchards, here, Tuscany, Germany, pineapple plantations in Hawaii, the friendly people of Toronto, all took a seat for the morning lecture, listening, taking notes, doodling hearts, or I love you notes to send to erase the nights of porn and the ill feeling afterwards, not for me, so long ago.

He could feel a shadow move, or a ray of light support a leaf. He talked with the cats and missed that 43-yard field goal by two inches, no hit the champs, and caught the runner from 30 yards, no touchdown today, it's my time to shine!

*

Wallace was glad to get back home, and at work, to discuss with Jake and his lab people about implementing some of the technology associated with LTE, or Long-Term Evolution, which the ladies in San Francisco told him about. This could increase transmitting speeds for all their devices, especially the one he wanted to talk about today, the 641.

"Problems?" he asked.

"Patent protection will be an issue. We'll have to obtain a license agreement for limited access," Jake said.

"After we try it let's move on it," Henson says. "Tommy, what do you think?" he asks his chief engineer.

"With what you sent over; we may not need it. We're fast now, and for this, I'm not sure it's that great of an application. You all will have to study the accessibility, but I'm not sure it's worth it in retail. They all have cameras now that are producing great results," he offers.

"You may be right, Jake?"

"I don't think it's worth it. But if I may, have you heard that Weapons Eye Sync is going up for sale?"

"No, I had not! That may be an answer. Get me what you can, and we'll discuss it. I'll give Thomas Robinson a call," Henson says. "Do you know his partner, Bruce Walker?" he asks Jake.

"Casually."

"I'll get the two of you together. Tommy, you know about them, right? They've used some of our conductors in the past?"

"I do. Great company, great products. Good works," he answers. "I'll get my team to look this over and let you know what we come up with."

"Let's all meet in three hours, back here in my office."

"Sure," Jake answers.

"10-4," Tommy responds.

*

Thomas had slept 20 hours, and was waking, groggy and confused. His expensive watch was missing, and he wasn't sure where he was. He looked at the fellow in the other bed and was alarmed at his dopey facial expression. He asked him what time it was anyway.

"Medication. Time for your medication. Breakfast in 20 minutes," he reports, then looks away. He looked back and said "You had a nice watch; Frankie got your watch. You may have to fight him to get it back. Give me a dollar and I will help you," he says.

Thomas didn't respond, still trying to make sense of where he was. He was still sleepy, but remembered being at a train station, but not much else. The clinical assistant knocked on the door, and came in.

"Good morning," she says, chipper and alert. "Time to get up; vital signs," she says. "Hi, my name is Sheila, good morning Mr. Robinson; feeling better?" she asks in a general way.

"Yes. Where am I?" he earnestly asks.

"Stabilization unit."

"Stabilization for what?" he asks.

"Oh, you don't remember. The nurse will explain everything. Go get in line for your vitals. Let's go," she snaps.

He was in shorts and a tee, and still confused about what all this meant. He looked at his roommate, who pulled on some pants and went out the door, behind Sheila. He then looked around for some pants and a shirt nearby, on the bed, but didn't see any. He opened the top, then middle drawer of his nightstand cabinet and saw a shirt, and a pair of pants he recognized. There were these paper foot protectors under the bed, but no shoes.

"This couldn't be jail," he thought. Before he could get dressed there was another knock at the door.

"Dr. Leland, may I come in?" The doctor entered the room and closed the door behind him.

"Mr. Thomas Robinson?" he speaks.

"Yes."

"Frazier Leland, Doctor of Psychiatry. How are you feeling?" he asks as he offers his right hand.

"Doctor, who, why, what?" Thomas can hardly speak or get his thoughts together. He does, however, pull on his pants, and puts on the shirt. "Doctor, help me out here, what's happened?"

*

"Weapons Eye Sync, how may I direct your call?"

"Thomas Robinson please."

"He's not available, would you like to leave a message?"

"Bruce Walker?"

"One moment please," she answers, then rings him.

"Bruce Walker."

"Mr. Walker, this is Wallace Henson of Henson Technologies; how are you today?"

"Fine."

"We met in Germany a couple of years ago, The Daylight Security sales meeting."

"Oh yeah, Henson; how are you these days?"

"Fine, fine. The reason I'm calling is that I hear WES is going on the block soon?"

"Yes. We're headed that way."

"Well I'm interested."

"That's good. We're proud of what we've done. Mr. Robinson has done some great things here. Oh, I remember now, I think we've used some of your chips in our devices."

"Correct sir. Where can I get the information?"

"Brewer, Moore, and Brown, they're the law firm handling the transaction. Is there anything I can do for you, now?"

"When will Mr. Robinson be available, I'd love to meet with you guys again?"

"Soon. It's 1.6 million to look over the books."

"Sure, no problem. Am I first in line?"

"Not sure. Contact the attorneys and get back with us."

"Okay, thanks, I will."

"Okay, see you soon."

After Wallace hangs up he thinks, "That was strange. Let me see what I can find out."

*

"You've had a psychotic break," the doctor tells Thomas.

"What does that mean exactly," Thomas asks, becoming more focused.

"You've not been yourself lately, or rather the self you've been is not good."

"Okay."

"We need to get you stabilized, and onto the treatment unit."

"What does that mean doctor?" Thomas asks.

"We'll try some medication to get you focused, and some mental therapy to help with your thinking process and participation with others on the unit in some directed activities to get a regular schedule going and to help you revive."

"What does all this mean doc?"

"Let's just say you have some mental issues that need proper resolution."

"Okay, I'm with you," he responds.

"A couple more questions, okay, and then you can get some rest."

"Okay."

"From what I understand your company has been doing some race-based research and product development. Is that right?"

Thomas gives him a confused look but doesn't answer.

"And I understand you've been gambling quite a bit for the past two months. Is that right?" the doctor asks him, as he continues to make notes on his electronic pad.

Again, the confused, blank stare from Thomas.

"Okay, staff will be taking your vital signs, get you some breakfast, and I've ordered some medication to help you get focused. I want you to relax and if you need something let staff know," the doctor reports. "Again, I'm Dr. Frazier Leland and I'll see you tomorrow."

The doctor taps a note on his pad, nods goodbye, and exits the room.

Chapter Twenty-Nine

"Shirley, this is Mary; how are you doing?" spoken with genuine concern.

"I'm okay, but this is strange. I saw it coming and I didn't act sooner, or rather differently," she answers. "I guess this is the big three for our age group, dementia, racist views, and gambling! How does such a smart man deteriorate so quickly? I guess we can throw in jealousy as well. And now this hospital stuff, visiting is tonight, and I don't want to go back there; seeing him like that is so hard," she says as she begins to weep.

Mary listens.

"I know. Thomas, before all this, had said Bruce had backed away from him somewhat and he didn't know what to do. Do you think that's the only reason they're selling the company?" Shirley asks.

"Well I think Bruce, actually, they both probably weren't enjoying it much anymore, but the racial views were tough to take. Even though they have a lot of good history, a black guy has become one of Bruce's best friends," Mary reports.

"I don't know what to do. I'm meeting with his counselor before visiting, and maybe she will have some answers, or at least some suggestions," Shirley says, with a hint of defeatism.

"Would you like me to go with you?" Mary asks.

"I could probably use a friend right now. That'd be great."

"Of course, what time?" Mary asks.

"About 5:30; she needs to complete the assessment we started when he was admitted. Visiting starts at 7:00," Shirley offers.

"Sure, that's fine. Just include me where I'm needed, but I don't need to know everything."

"That's okay, we don't need to have any secrets," Shirley gives.

"We can leave at 4:45. That should give us enough time," Mary says.

"Okay, I'll meet you at your car then. Thanks."

*

The Avery Mental Health Institute was founded in 1976 by Drs. Raymond Chadwick and Donald Phillips, local psychiatrists who wanted to provide inpatient services to clients who wanted to be free of dependence on barbiturates and alcohol. They bought 30 acres of land in prominent northeast Atlanta and developed a first-rate facility with office space for consulting physicians, and other mental health practitioners. It quickly developed a reputation for caring and professional services, provided by a first-rate staff of nurses, counselors, and associated mental health disciplines. Their primary clients were upper class, and the well insured, as their fees were commensurate with the level of expertise recruited to work there. You could have a banker, a rock musician, a professional athlete, a CEOs' wife, or a worker from the local auto plant on the 15-person treatment unit. The Stabilization and Detox units were housed on separate wings of the hospital. The décor and furnishings throughout the building were state of the art for these types of developing facilities, hospital clean, environmentally comfortable, and clinically accommodating.

*

This was Harry Klinger's third individual session with Larry. Last session he talked about wanting to smoke a 'blunt' again.

"So, how's it going today, Mr. Klinger?" Larry begins.

"Much better this week. I did not smoke, and I don't want to smoke. I was feeling lonely and wanted to be with my old friends. Plus, I don't know what to do with Jessica; she's crazy!" he shares.

"Jessica's your girlfriend, right?"

"Yes sir. I love her, I think, but girls are ridiculous sometimes."

"What's different?"

"I think it's because I notice more things now. I'm afraid of some things, and I'm not as sure sometimes as I used to be. I don't know, I'm changing. Is this what happens when you stop smoking?"

"Sometimes. You started at 15 so a lot of your natural feelings got corrupted. You're what, oh, today's your 18th birthday; Happy Birthday."

"Yeah." Harry smiles broadly.

"So, as you're getting used to how you feel, you notice more about what others mean to you. Jessica's important to you and what she does is important, so now you have to get used to how she's dealing with her feelings, and her life, just like you."

"Is it the same?"

"No, and yes. You have to do the best you can with it."

"What do you mean?"

"Well like at work, you had to learn how to make a sandwich right? You knew how to make a sandwich at home, but now you make sandwiches for others. And they tell you what they want on it. It may not be what you would want, or think should go on the sandwich, but it's what they want. So you must give them that. Or otherwise you don't eat either."

They both laugh as Harry gets the pun.

"So Jessica is going to be and act the way she wants to act, and I have to accept that?"

"Yep, or not. But you don't have to approve or disapprove of everything she does."

"I get it."

"How's your dad?"

"He's good. He still can't believe I'm coming to see you for counseling, but he can tell it's helping me. How many more times should I come back?"

"Let's say two more. Now what about school?"

"Jessica and I enrolled at Georgia Perimeter, and we start in August."

"That's good. Maybe we can talk about that next week, along with anything else that comes up?"

"Okay sir, thanks."

*

At the morning staff meeting Henson wanted to review the follow up meeting from yesterday.

"So we're clear, let the 641 rest?"

"That's where I stand," Jake speaks up.

"It's a waste, sir. No money there." Tommy offers.

"Okay, Weapons Eye Sync, what'd you find out Jake?"

"Like we've already known, their products are the best on the market, and even though there's been a lull in sales performance, the next three to seven years are promising. They have some DOD contracts coming due in late 2012, and the big market police departments can't buy enough, only because of budgets constraints; and that should loosen with a couple of high-profile situations where an officer's actions are brought into question, for instance an unarmed person killed, or a mentally disturbed person pulling a 'suicide by cop' routine, or God forbid, a child is killed while playing with a gun," Jake reports. "The financials are solid. They were vague on several patent and copyright decisions, but Mr. Brewer assured me those would be cleared up before a sale could go through."

"Do we have a hard copy, and a digital one?" Henson asks.

"I read a digital summary after the wire went through. He's sending you a full copy. It should be here by four, and we will have a copy in our e-mails this evening," Jake says.

"Tommy, I'll forward a copy to you," Wallace says. "Okay, that's all I have for now. Jake, Tommy?"

"Do you want to see my proposal for Triple Line, and how we would use the skin color angle?" Jake says.

"Not yet, I want to sleep on what you gave me this morning. Plus, we've got an appointment with the bank tomorrow at 9:30am," Henson says. "Tommy, thanks for coming up."

"You know where to find me," Tommy says as he leaves the office.

"Jake, should we do this?" Wallace begins. "You know this will be your baby?"

"I think we should, but I do want to bring on some extra eyes to look over their past company profile, and four-year projections," Jake offers. "We need a team fluent in the German language with technical skills."

"What level?"

"Minimum master's level engineers, and a few Ph.D. types."

"Okay. Do what you need to do for the sake of the company. How about your personal staffing, do you have the right people in place?" Henson asks him.

"I did want to ask you about Herman Webb?" Jake asks.

"Herman's a player. He'll retire in two years, so keep him close, and use the hell out of him. He's paid very well."

"Okay, thanks."

"Jake, you're doing a great job, and I appreciate it. Have you finished your classes?"

"I have; tested, certified, and ready to go! Thank you, sir, for picking up the tab on those," Jake reports.

"You're welcome, and worth it. How's the family?" Henson asks.

"All's well there, thank you. On that note, sir, is there anything else you need from me?" Jake asks with a bit of caution.

"There could be something personal we need to go over soon, but I'll let you know," Wallace says.

"Okay, thanks," Jake responds.

Chapter Thirty

Helmut and Bruce continued the conversation in German for the accuracy of the technical descriptions. Daylight Security had bought exclusive rights to market and sell the LTE high-speed wireless technology for two years, which the CR2 unit relied upon for transmitting the collected data between cellular networks and the mobile devices. This gave advantage to the military for usage in combat theaters whereby commanders could not only determine the skill levels of the opponent but could also track individual movement of troops. There had been limited success in Iraq, and now more effective procedures had been adapted for use in Afghanistan. Estimates were for 10,000 civilian and military lives saved.

"Have you any other instances where the device did not register any data on a subject?" Helmut asks.

"No, we have not; only Mr. Fleming," Bruce answers.

"How about his brother?"

"No problem, he registered."

"What do your research people think is the reason for this?" Helmut asks.

"Dr. Taylor believes there is a genetic component similar to what evolves in world leaders," Bruce responds.

"How does she mean that?"

"Certain biological processes are masked, and others are enhanced related to IQ, blood pressure, and intent of action," Bruce relays to him.

"But not the brother?" Helmut asks with confusion.

"Like in some families one is an alcoholic, the other is not," Bruce explains.

"So, what world leaders have you scanned?" Conover asks.

"POTUS."

"What happened?"

"Same result as Mr. Fleming."

"So Larry Fleming is presidential material?" Helmut asks, sarcastically.

"Not so much that, but his ability to execute certain tasks is outstanding, at a presidential level. We could not find any references to what military operation he performed on May 13, 1973, but we know that all members of his platoon were killed, and a certain action, with possible destructive, international implications was prevented. My friends at the CIA go completely mum when his name is mentioned," Bruce reports to his associate.

Helmut Conover takes out a small piece of paper and writes 'Munich—-Beirut' on it, shows it to Bruce, then shreds it.

"Can we get a blood test?" Helmut asks.

"Not sure how," Bruce answers.

"His IQ?"

"His IQ in basic training was 121, but I'm not sure that's the operating score. I think he has a second gear that runs at least to 125," Bruce offers.

"Anything else?"

"Records were lost in a fire in a warehouse in Missouri back in the late 70s," Bruce gives him.

"So who is this guy really?" Helmut ponders aloud.

"We really don't know."

*

"Hi, I'm Joana Washington, Family Therapist. Mrs. Robinson?"

"Yes, and this is my neighbor, Mrs. Mary Walker," Shirley says to the middle-aged woman.

"Come on back," she says as she opens the hallway door leading to her office.

Joana is a 47-year-old, LCSW, who's been in family counseling for 19 years. She is neatly dressed, well kept up, and cordial. Her office has adequate space for a desk and chair, a love seat, and two padded folding chairs. Mary and Shirley sit together on the bench. Once they get comfortable Shirley gets a tissue from her purse and begins to cry a little.

"It's okay," Mary says, putting an arm around her shoulder.

Meanwhile Joana is looking over a chart, takes a sip of water from a glass, and looks over at them.

"It's okay," she mirrors Mary. "These things are never easy, having a loved one here," she starts. "I'd like to finish the assessment and talk a little as we go along. Obviously, you're comfortable with Mary being here for this, Mrs. Robinson, is that correct?" she asks.

"This is all new, but yes, no secrets between us now," Shirley offers and smiles warmly towards Mary.

"So, some gambling, racist rants, business owner, okay, how have y'all been, the relationship?" She asks Shirley.

"His business requirements have been stressful, the racist stuff is hard to live with at times, but the gambling has been detrimental to our ability to have a decent conversation for the past two months. There's like a wall between us now. Hiring the private detective to follow him was sneaky, but I did want to get an idea of how bad it was. The $20,000.00 was not a problem, just that funny look he would have on his face when he came home. I didn't know who he was anymore."

"Meals together, going out to things, sexual relations the past six months?" Joana asks her.

"We've been together 23 years. Not as much sex, and it hasn't been fun lately; we still go out, and there are times when it's still wonderful. I think we still love each other. We went on a business trip to Amsterdam two years ago and he had to kill a man, he probably saved my life, and many others, I think he changed after that. Some of his work in the past, with the government, was top secret, and of course certain aspects of his business he had to protect, so I don't know, but as I'm talking I think that changed him somewhat, killing that man."

"Alcohol, drug use? Oh, do you have kids?" Joana adds to the question.

Shirley looks to Mary, and her eyes fill up with fluids and turn red. She starts a full on tearful, crying spell. Through the tears, she begins: "No drugs that I know of," she pauses. "We rarely drink. We have no kids together; I got pregnant in college. I gave her up for adoption. I've never heard from her, and I don't know where she went. It was with my boyfriend of a year, Randall, a black man. We had broken up, and I never told him."

Shirley breaks free of Mary's embrace and stands. She twirls around in the office and stops crying. She blows her nose, and looks at Mary, then Joana.

"I've never told Thomas, and I don't think he knows," she says.

Joana starts to offer a comment but waits. Shirley studies a watercolor painting on the wall ahead of her, squints, and reads the title card, 'Spring Light' by Jodi Dixon. Mary continues to listen and feels the power of what was just revealed in the room.

*

It was day four, and Thomas was clearing, his conversations were more coherent as he was responding favorably to the medication, and he had gotten his watch back from Frankie, who had to be rushed to the ER with a head concussion, probably from a fall. He had not talked to Shirley since being admitted, though he knew today she would be here for visiting. He was getting along well with his doctor and was more sociable with the other patients on the unit, as far as that would go, as most were still in the throes of a mental crisis. Bits of memory were accessible now, and somewhat disturbing, but overall, he was feeling better.

*

Mary decided to go sit in the lobby and wait, as Joana walked with Shirley the thirty yards to the stabilization unit. The door to the unit was electronically opened by a staff member because it was more secure that way, even though Joana had her keys. As they walked in, Shirley could see Thomas sitting out in the day room and became sad for him. He could see her now as well, and he smiled. Joana took Shirley to a small conference room and went back out to get Thomas. They came back, and Thomas and Shirley hugged warmly and held on to each other for a few extra seconds. Joana stood by smiling, then asked them to sit, by hand gesture, so they could get started with a short meeting before they had their visiting time.

"How are you darling?" Shirley asks.

"Getting better," Thomas responds.

"Mr. Robinson you've had a rough ride lately, anything you'd like to share, or any questions?" Joana asks.

"Much is still blurry, and I'm trying to adjust to being here. The staff is attentive, and great. And I like the doctor," he says.

"I'd like to go over a few things and then you all can visit a while," Joana mentions.

Thomas and Shirley nod in acknowledgement.

"I'd like to pursue a couple of questions, and you all set the boundaries. They'll be concerning your care and follow-up Mr. Robinson. Your wife and I met earlier and went over a few details about what happened, but I have a couple more questions for the both of you," she says.

Shirley becomes a little tense as she hopes the social worker is discreet.

"Mr. Robinson how are you feeling right now, mentally?"

"I'm still a little shaken, and not totally clear as to what's happening. I do know I'm in a psych hospital, and that something went wrong with my usual behavior. Dementia is that what the doctor said at the other place?" he questions.

They both look at Shirley who's lost in her own thoughts.

"Oh, yes, we had a neurological work-up done recently, two weeks ago, and it seems Thomas has a mild case of dementia," she says. "We have medication, but he's resistant to taking it."

"Why is that Mr. Robinson?" Joana asks.

"I'm not sure I understand the question," Thomas offers as an answer.

Joana pauses a moment before speaking.

"Mrs. Robinson, good to meet you. Thomas, we'll talk tomorrow. You all should have a little visit now. We'll know more after the doctor sees him in the morning," she directs to Shirley. "Let me take you out to the day room, and the nurse will give further instructions about visiting, and anything the doctor has ordered in the way of therapy, and what's next," Joana shares.

Shirley says thank you and follows her out to the day room; Thomas looks puzzled as he walks beside Shirley.

*

Mary remained quiet as they got into the car and drove off. She allowed Shirley to be with her thoughts and feelings as obviously this was an overwhelming shot of life experience, and maybe Thomas was not as improved as hoped. Even though the sharing about her love child seemed to roll off her lips that had to be momentous. Mary would assure her, at some point, that information would be held in strict confidence. Shirley's patrician-like carriage and looks were being tested in new ways now. Trust and friendship must be inviolate at this time.

"Mary," she began, "whatever you wish to share with Bruce is fine by me, I don't wish to have any secrets now; discretion, yes."

"Shirley, of course. Thank you," Mary answered.

"He's not well. Better, but not well."

They ride the rest of the way home in silence.

Chapter Thirty-One

Jake lands in St. Louis about 10am. He gets his rental car and drives the 27 miles to Rockdale, a suburb just east of the big city. He pulls into the police department lot and is met outside by his grow-up pal Leslie Thompson, the Police Chief for the 80-person squad here. They greet each other warmly and go into the building and to Leslie's office, a mixture of notebooks, newspapers, various gadgets that work, or not, and a large picture of his wife Susan, and their two kids, Ellen, and Roy. Leslie is straight out of central casting, 6'2", 230 lbs., full faced, rugged, and eyes that move about swiftly. A veteran of Iraq and Afghanistan, with two shoulder wounds, he commands respect and cooperation from his staff. They exchange pleasantries about family, and old times from childhood, then Jake gets to the reason for his visit.

"The 1027BH device, your assessment?" Jake asks him.

"Good tool. Man, it tells you a lot about a suspect, some of these boys out here can't believe it. It's fast and clean, no misfires," he offers.

"Which version do you use now?" Jake asks him.

"Let's see, that box, right over there. Hand it to me, or you can read it, what does it say?"

"Second Generation, 2011," Jake reads aloud.

"Yeah, we got them back in the spring, just after that big mess with that boy who shot Jeremy. Thank God he survived. Man, when my guys hit the streets they knew who was carrying and what, their ability and their intent to harm. We cleaned the streets and kept a riot from happening. We had the evidence, so when the feds came down after that big shot lawyer came prancing around down here, what a bull shitter, we kept the peace. Even the black folks were happy about it. Some people just wanted a riot, tear up shit, get on TV, it's a shame watching those youngsters running into stores, taking other people's stuff. They could work, or at least stay home. Anyway, sorry about that, it just makes me mad the way some people think they're supposed to act stupid at certain times. You remember Tommy Green and them; they didn't act like that. His family came from slaves too. He runs a machine shop now over in Bremen, Tennessee, family business, you know, the good stuff like us. But anyway, it's a great product, this high-tech stuff is great. Why?" he asks.

"We're thinking about buying the company that makes them," Jake says simply.

"Man that's cool. Good stuff: when are you going to bring Marie and the kids out this way?" Leslie asks him.

"When we buy the company I'll bring the family, and hand deliver your first order. How about that!" Jake says.

"That's a good deal. All right let me go back to work. Anything else?" he asks.

Jake retrieves a box from his briefcase, and hands it to Leslie.

"This is their latest, the CR2. This thing will do everything but give you a shave! Try it out, and let me know what you think, within a week if possible," Jake asks.

"I'll give it to Donovan, our tech guy. He works the mall. He has stuff going on every day. I'll text you or something. Thanks buddy," Leslie says.

"Okay, thanks."

Jake begins his journey back east.

*

Bruce is reading a newspaper when Mary comes in. He gets up and greets her.

"How is Shirley, and how did it go at the hospital?" he asks.

"It's a mess doc," she says playfully. "Thomas is better, but there are issues that will probably take a while to uncover. I did not go back to the unit with her, so I didn't see him, but by the way she closed up when we left, it must have been scary," she says.

"Well, the business is running itself, so I don't have much to do. We have some solid offers, so the sale should go smoothly," Bruce reports.

"You'll need him sane, won't you?"

"Not really; he's signed off on most everything already, and the attorneys are attending to the legalities," he says.

"You're mighty laid back about it all?" she observes.

"It's because I'm in love with you!" he says.

"Ahhh. I love you too. So, hungry?" she asks.

"I will be after we make love," he says will a grin.

"Okay!" she responds.

Chapter Thirty-Two

Johnny Hyber was out walking, a free man for the first time in 18 years. Johnny did 16-years federal time for distribution of crack cocaine, was out eight weeks, and was returned to prison for making terroristic threats. Prison had hardened him, and he was still angry at Larry Fleming for what happened 40 years ago in that warehouse over on Chapel Road. Larry had set up the deal, but Johnny put too much cut on the dope, diminishing its strength. Joe Jenkins was a heroin addict, but Johnny didn't know that, thinking he could pass it off. When Joe pulled out his 'works' and fixed up a hit Larry left, so when the dope didn't do what was promised Joe and his boy beat up Johnny and took the dope, half a 'key.' So of course Johnny's money was way short when it was time to pay for the dope that had been fronted to him by Smooth Head. He had to scramble by selling two cars, and a favorite piece of jewelry to save his life. Johnny had never forgiven Larry for leaving him like that and wanted to talk to him now, even though there was really nothing to settle.

Darlene and Larry were asleep when the light blinked twice, waking Larry immediately. The loud, crashing sound of the glass and wood paneled back door being battered sent him on high alert, and he reached for the CR2 device Leroy had given him: 'AK-47, intent to harm, stupid, very skilled, blood pressure high', was the read out on the screen. He touched Darlene forcefully, pushing her to the edge of the king-sized bed, waking her so she was able to slowly roll off to the floor. Larry jumped up, reached for the spray, and broke open the side window. He tumbled out, rushed past the row of flowering crepe myrtles, rushed to the back door, and set off the fuse that blew up the dining room. Johnny was knocked down, lost control of the assault rifle, and Larry was on him before he fully regained consciousness. Johnny tried to get up and Larry pushed him back to the rubble on the floor, burned and dazed. Larry picked up the weapon, rushed to the bedroom to make sure Darlene was okay, and went back to find Johnny had passed out.

*

Wallace Henson had come up with the figure of I.438 Billion Dollars for the purchase of Weapons Eye Sync, its subsidiary Premium Photo, and all patents, copyrights, and existing licensure agreements. Jake had signed off on the offer, with some questions about the life of certain aspects of a co-joined patent registration. He hoped it wouldn't entail any legal entanglements. Their lawyers had assured them the language was adequate for complete ownership by WES, and thus the buyer. The package was presented to Brewer, Moore, and Brown on December 12, 2011, at 10:00am.

He and Linda had spent the weekend in Miami and had sex. The ambiguity of their relationship continued as she didn't know whether she was a high-priced whore, a gold digger, an administrative assistant with benefits, or what? Her feelings for him were a mixed bag, and when he called outside business hours, or needed a companion, like now, for a trip, she could never say no. For his part, sober or not, he depended on her. If it was love, he wasn't aware. He'd was sober now for eight months and had enjoyed their walks on the beach and the food at the Cuban style restaurant. He felt relaxed, and generally felt good about being with her, but not as a steady girlfriend, even though this relationship had gone on, such as it was, for years now.

Linda stayed over with Wallace at his condo in Midtown Atlanta Sunday night and their lovemaking was more passionate than ever. They both explored intimate ways to pleasure the other, giving, stroking, laughing, wanting to trust that the time they've known each other would give way to this fresh experience. They kissed in new places and asked for what they needed. Time passed, and the embraces became wetter, stronger, filled with a longing they'd never expressed, or knew they had. Each was coming alive to the other, warmly accepting there was a reason they've kept the relationship ongoing, undefined, yet so true, never spoken, but always felt.

*

The stabilization unit nurse's station was in a horseshoe shaped configuration, so the full area could be monitored by sight, as well as camera, to keep the 10 patients as safe as possible. The three hundred or so, square feet area had all resources within easy reach so that charts, emergency medical supplies, reference books, and workstation space could be shared by doctors, social workers, techs, and the nurses on duty, with a good flow and level of comfort for all. A thick, hardened plastic partition rose about four feet above the counter tops and connected to aluminum braces to withstand attempts by out of control, or angry patients who could harm staff if no barrier were there. The entrance door was braced as well. Thelma Ashford was the day charge nurse, and commanded the station like a field general, making calls, taking doctors' orders, arranging family sessions, transportation, you name it, if it happened on this unit Thelma was aware of it. She would arrive in the morning at 6:45, take shift report from the overnight staff, do rounds with her staff, and sit in her swivel chair, barking directions until lunch time for her, about 12:30, when she would eat, check with her family at home, take a potty break, and return to her post, and work until 2:45, when she would meet with the evening shift for report.

She was a 'big mama,' about 5'9", 220 lbs. and surely had an IQ comparable to anyone who would come on the unit, as she could converse with patients, doctors, counselors, maintenance staff, whomever. The one patient to give her a run for her money was Joel Taylor, a Vietnam veteran, 82nd Airborne, who had become a crack addict in his fifties, after making a ton of money building custom homes near East Ferry Rd. Joel clocked in at about 140 and was probably bi-polar before it became popular. They had a conversation once in his room, two days after he was admitted, that should have been recorded for training purposes:

"I don't think you understand why I'm here this morning," he said.

"I don't; you're far too smart."

"I should be, but the crack makes me smarter, and I can't control it."

"Why would you want to control it?"

"So the helicopters won't find me, and I don't run out of money."

"Is that a problem?"

"Only on Saturdays, after night watch, and I don't get relieved on time by the C.O. when the brothers want to go clubbing and stop selling."

"Do you sell it?"

"Only to the foot soldiers, the ones doing hand to hand combat on the streets, the nickel and dimers."

"You mean $5, $10 worth?"

"Light weights. Before the white boys come. They can come to my house, and buy O.Z.s. The cops won't arrest them."

"Are you the only white person in your neighborhood?"

"The only one that hangs out. The rest ride by in their Super Cars."

"So you walk around?"

"When I have to."

"Do you want to stop?"

"No."

"Why are you here?"

"The helicopters: this is a secure building."

Joel was gritty, with a ruggedly handsome face, and a manic smile as he talked. Thelma knew she was outmatched with this one as he was just beginning to come around.

*

"Hey! How you doing, sweetie?" Darla greeted as Darlene answered the phone.

"Darla! Just thinking about you! What's up?" Darlene responds.

"Hey. Everything's going well. How's that good-looking man you live with?"

"You know, Larry's just cool. When are you coming back home?"

"You know y'all need to come out here, get some open air, some desert love!" Darla says.

"You're probably right. How long has it been?"

"Four years now; can you believe it?"

"I can't. Dating?"

"Some of these cowboys are all right, but it's a challenge. Doug was my man. It's going to take a lot to top him," Darla offers.

"I know that's right girl!" Darlene says. "What's new?"

"You know it's great. I've opened a little jewelry shop, with some wall art, cards, you know, something to play around with. It pays the rent, keeps me in coffee money. Meeting a lot of people, tourists, and such. And the locals have been good to me," she says.

"I tell you what, let me get with Larry, it's been too long, we do need to come back to New Mexico. Are you still target shooting?" she says.

"Not much, but I keep sharp, you know."

"Okay, love you. Thanks for calling. Soon."

"Yes, if not I'm coming back to get cha! Love ya!" Darla says. They both have a good laugh before hanging up.

*

Jack Moran had simply played the cards he was dealt. He was a good soldier and was a product of his environment, and the times. He rose to a good level of productivity and skill development but got caught up in the 'winds of change' as it were. Even though the paper he wrote back in the 1980s was quite prescient, and his descriptions of certain cultural lifestyle excesses were on target, he missed the importance of the young senator's heritage, and destiny. No one else had a flow chart, or algorithm to predict it either. And thus, after 35 years of, in one sense, admirable service, he will be retired soon.

Chapter Thirty-Three

"Jake, this is the only problem I see with the CR2. It relates to the updates Daylight Security challenged, saying skin color recognition was copyrighted, not patented, by them in 2010. They've been one of our best business partners and I'm not sure what Helmut's trying to do. Based on the legal opinion, and it will be a part of the sales agreement, you should be fine. See attached. As a matter of fact, I've read their patent list, and reviewed the drawings, and they're reaching. See you Monday, Bruce."

Attachment:

RE: Weapons Eye Sync/CR2 Unit

Petitioner did not receive federal clearance to sell an updated version of their 1027BH device, nor did it seek agency approval for the redesign when it began selling in 2011. Clearance is required for all 'substantive' updates to devices.

The Lower Court had ruled "It's not clear if it was a 'substantive' update."

Signed, Roland Harris, Dir.

*

Thomas was standing, looking out the front side window where the road was. He could look through the trees, and occasionally see a few deer walking together about 10:30 some mornings, looking for food, or frolicking about. This was the main road, and traffic could be noticed at times, especially in the evenings when the aftercare, or 12 step meetings were held. Staff members would be seen walking past as well going from the main hospital building to the conference center for trainings. It all seemed foreign to him as he couldn't connect his thinking to what was happening outside, or inside, for that matter, as he still wasn't clear on why he was here, or what it meant. When Shirley would come visit he felt good, but didn't always remember who she was, even though she gave him the dollar he asked for two weeks ago.

Shirley was becoming more bewildered at his decline but was gaining a greater appreciation for why her father held the profession in such awe and didn't over emphasize how helpful he could be to patients. He was a great diagnostician, not a therapist, and he respected the limits of what chemistry and understanding could do in the way of restoration of damaged neurological process. He had admired the talents expressed in therapeutic discourse by knowing, caring, and nuanced counselors when expected results were realized. The best doctors respected the limits and strengths of medical training and knew there were other forces at work.

"Mr. Robinson, your doctor is here to see you," spoke Sheila.

"Okay." Thomas turned slowly and followed her to the small conference room.

*

Larry and Darlene were enjoying the walk around downtown Atlanta. The air was crisp, and students had a brisk pace passing by going to class, or wherever. The sun was bright, and as they professed their ongoing love for each other they couldn't help but reminisce about their college days, and the other times of socialization with peers of other races. As usual, Larry had the dual notations of place and time.

"Summer, 1976, on this spot next to Woodruff Park I shook Jimmie Carter's hand, eight years later I gave away $300.00 worth of clothes for a bag of fake weed. 10 years after that I was working on the 17th floor of the old First National Tower counseling probationers for Trainer Services. Summer of 1974 I kissed a white girl in the parking lot of Lenox Square Mall, 37 years later I'm here with my African Queen, the love of my life. Summer of 1971 I snatched a bag of weed from a white hippie, 40 years later I'm counseling their son, or granddaughter. It goes on and on," Larry recounted.

"It's so funny because my life was so culturally specific. Walked to school in the neighborhood, Washington High, Spelman up the street. Worked for Trust Citizens Bank while in school, and now working for a small black owned workforce agency. Never dated a white guy, or other." They both laugh at the label. "It was pretty sterile until I met you," she comments.

They looked around at some of the buildings, or spaces where buildings had been, new names, new companies, new people. Metropolitan Atlanta had become a world city, and the old black/white references didn't hold true when addressing crime, or residential development. Money, convenience, and exposure dictated where you could go, and with whom you would ride.

"Ever wished we had moved back into the city?" Darlene asked Larry.

"No. I still like driving in for meals and movies, meeting our friends, watching the young folks move about on the city dance floor, jogging, hustling, and discovering all the living angles afforded them with an urban experience here. Not too messy, not too hard. How about you?" he asks her.

"I kind of miss it. But like you I'm glad we get to drive away."

*

"Mr. Robinson how are you today?" Doctor Leland asks as he enters the room.

"Fine."

"Time, place, experience, where are you, now?"

"A good place. Why did they move my roommate?"

"He made a mistake and hurt somebody."

"Oh."

"Do you want to try the other unit, and see if you can move around better, talk to some other people?"

"Okay."

The doctor looks over some notes in his chart.

"See if you can follow this: Appetite is good, vitals remain stable, not very talkative, doesn't ask for, or seem to know what he needs, sleeps seven hours, naps once or twice a day, cannot recall why he's in the hospital, how long he's been here, or have any notion about treatment. 14% regression. Dr. Singh. 11/17/11."

"What does that mean?" Thomas asks.

Dr. Leland feels his phone vibrate.

"Mr. Robinson, I've got an emergency, and I'll come back later to go over some options the treatment team has discussed for your ongoing care. Okay?"

"Okay," he answered, with a flat affect.

*

Wallace and Linda woke with a nice glow, feeling that the relationship had perhaps moved a bit, leading to a different trust level. They ordered breakfast in from a kitchen up the street, and lazily allowed the early morning to progress. Wallace was fighting an urge to call the office, or find Jake, and resisted, knowing that basically all the business features were in good hands. Within a couple of weeks, he should hear if the deal closed, and he wanted to stay second to Jake on this one. He looked dreamily into her eyes, and they fondled, and caressed each other playfully. Linda wondered if this would move her to a 'kept' woman status, or just keep her on the payroll with different duties. At this moment he was not requiring any nursing skill care because of his sobriety, but she'd seen it too often before when he would start drinking, not be able to stop, and would require a physical detox regimen again. She hoped and prayed that he'd stay sober, and perhaps fulfill her as only a true partner could. Wallace was having some of the same hopes, and thoughts, but dared not to allow himself to let go all the way, "She works for me," was all he could allow emotionally.

Chapter Thirty-Four

"Mr. Fleming, may I take the story home again, Jessica and I want to read it together? She says it reminds her of what she was like when she was 15 years old," Harry Klinger mentioned.

"Sure. Which character do you relate to?" Larry asks him.

"Both. I understand Gregory a little, but the descriptions Gloria makes about what it's like to smoke weed are right on," he says. "I've never really talked to a black girl that much, so I don't know much about the race stuff that way; but Jessica does, so that's why she wants to read it again. She said she liked a black dude for a while, and sat with him at the school cafeteria sometimes, but it wasn't like dating, or anything."

"What do you think about that?" Larry asks him.

"I don't think they kissed or anything, so it's all right," he says.

"Okay, good. Here's the story." Larry hands him the folder with the seven-page story in it. "I guess we'll wrap up next week?" Larry says to him.

"Sure, you know my daddy wants to come. Is that all right?" Harry asks.

Larry pauses for a moment, not sure if this is a setup of some kind, or really a supportive thing, father, and son, together.

"Sure, have him call me before the session next week."

"Okay, I'll tell him. It'll be a trip!" Harry says, excitedly.

"Yeah, okay, sure. Have a good week. See y'all then," Larry says.

"Okay, thanks sir."

Chapter Thirty-Five

Shirley arrived at the hospital about 9:45 Friday morning, December 9. Thomas was being discharged after a brief exit conference. Thomas was speaking with Dr. Scott when she arrived.

"Come on in, I'm Dr. Denise Scott, Psychologist, and we were just beginning to review your husband's progress," she says.

Thomas stands and embraces Shirley, who gives him a soft peck on the right cheek. "You look well darling," she observes.

"Let's all have a seat and go over a few things," Dr. Scott says, as Thomas and Shirley stare at each other, not really paying attention to the doctor. "Thomas, would you like to start?" she offers.

"Why yes, thank you. Darling, I owe you a tremendous apology for my recent behavior, prior to coming into the hospital. The gambling, the ranting, the accusations, all a part of some misguided thinking which I can correct. The physical diagnosis, we'll deal with appropriately as I've had time to adjust to this aspect of aging. I guess the word 'dementia' just freaked me out. So, we'll have to do what's necessary. Lastly, I love you very much."

Shirley sobs softly and hugs the man she loves. "I love you too darling. We'll be okay."

*

The law offices of White, Farmer, and White are located on the thirtieth floor of The Halo Tower. The firm was founded back in 1959 by Ronald and Cedric White, brothers from Athens, Georgia. Mr. Farmer became a partner in 1967, shortly after the Professional Football Team was up and running. There are 90 lawyers who work out of this office, which occupies this, and the thirty-first floor as well. Another office is in Houston, with a team of 40 lawyers. They specialize in mergers and acquisitions, and Sally Penfield is a major player, having moved here from Dallas in 2002, after managing what could have been a terrible loss for a certain politically connected food purveyor. She is bright, seasoned, and articulate, and the daughter of Aaron Penfield, who was in federal custody for stock manipulation, and who had been an attorney of note himself. He has since killed a fellow inmate at the prison and will probably never see the free world again. Her mother died last year. She is married to Jayson Hunter, also an attorney. They have four kids and live here in Buckhead.

"Are you going to be able to wrap up the Henson, Weapons Eye Sync deal today?" Mr. Cedric White asked her in the early morning planning meeting.

"We may. I have some documents from a firm in Germany that needed a ruling, and I should have that by nine," she responds.

"Do we have all the wires in?" he further asks.

"Not as of midnight. A transfer on behalf of Mr. Henson is pending. Ahmm, 80 million dollars is somewhere, and I hope to have confirmation by nine as well."

"Good. Anything else?" he asks her.

"Are you sitting in or Ronald," she asks.

"Ronald knows both parties, so he would be helpful. Oh, here's a note for you from him."

"Okay, thanks."

"Thank You. Good luck."

*

"Should we go back, or forward?" Thomas asks Shirley as she turns onto the main street.

"Back a little, then forward," she says.

"Who goes first?" he asks her.

"Maybe I should, and maybe this is too early, but I need to share this with you."

Thomas became stern in posture and looked directly ahead.

"While in college I dated a black guy for about a year. It was nice, and we did a lot, and I learned a lot. His family accepted me and that was good. My parents were more reserved about the whole thing, and daddy only wished me well, perhaps knowing that it wouldn't last. It was ending about the time I first saw you when I worked part time in the mail room at the precinct. I became pregnant by him, and had the baby, a little girl that I gave up for adoption. He never knew, and I didn't tell him. I don't know what happened to her after that. It was a decision I made, and I don't regret it. Of course that's been a very long time ago. I probably should have told you this once we started getting serious, but I never considered it a problem. Perhaps I was wrong."

Thomas sits with this for a few moments, then turns to look at her. She looks back at him briefly as the traffic flow was heavy.

"When I was in the eighth grade, and integration was just starting, two black boys tried to take a quarter from me one afternoon after school. I put my right hand in the pocket of my pants and kept it there as they tried to pull my arm back and away. I was determined not to let that happen, and it didn't, even though they beat me up a little, nothing much. I vowed then those black mother..., I'm sorry, I'm not going there anymore, that those kids would not take my money, ever! And I guess I've been holding on to that quarter ever since."

Their eyes water, and Shirley decides to turn down a side street and park. They sit, and cry, and hold each other for twenty minutes.

*

Jake and Marie were enjoying becoming more active in the community church. It was a diverse congregation of about 600, and she ran the cash register downstairs after the Sunday service, collecting the $10.00 per adult, and $5.00 per kid cost for the usually generous meal. Jake helps with Sunday School, maintaining the classrooms, and making sure there are enough books on hand for the three different age groups: children, young adult, and adult. He rarely teaches a class but will if someone can't make it. Their kids also seem happy there as they have developed friendships and help when asked to perform a chore.

About an hour after church, when they got home, Jake's phone vibrates, and he looks at the screen. It was Linda saying Wallace was sober but having a bad day. 'Please call ASAP.' Jake excused himself to the den and called Linda.

"Hello."

"Hey Linda, Jake."

"Good, thanks for calling. We're at his condo here in town, and he talked of drinking, but didn't. He's nervous about tomorrow. He's resting now, but I'll call you back as soon as he's awake; I know he wants to talk to you," she reports to him.

"That sounds good. I'm at home, and I'll be available the rest of the day. Let him know that as soon as he wakes."

"I will, thanks."

Chapter Thirty-Six

"Jake how are you doing Buddy?" Wallace says.

"I'm good boss, talk to me."

"Jake, back in 2010 I cut a deal with some DOD folks who were not on the up and up and it took a back-door payment of 19 million dollars to get me out of a bad business, and life-threatening situation. It was off the books, and I don't think you'll hear from them ever, but I'll give you their names, histories, and where they can be found. Now, this has left us about 20 million dollars short on the deal tomorrow, and I've got a call in to my first cousin, Alice, who's in Hawaii, who I may be able to get to finance that amount for Henson Technologies through a fabric firm she owns. The only problem is that Freddie, my nephew, is a convicted felon, and handles her affairs here on the mainland. We have a good relationship, but you see where this is going, he can't be in the picture at all. We may have to delay the closing, and either you or I may need to fly to the island to talk to her. I'll know something in about an hour," Wallace reports.

"Okay, just let me know," Jake responds.

"I will, but I need to keep you away from too much information so that when you're asked certain tough questions you really won't know what happened, okay. Actually, there is one thing; do you have any friends in Germany?"

"I do. I have a pal who lives near Mainz," he says.

"Good. I'll get back to you on that as well. Look, I know Linda called, and I hit a rough patch, but I'm okay. It's almost nine months, and I'm getting used to this sober thing, okay."

"Thanks. Keep me informed," Jake says.

Jake didn't quite know what to make of all this. Was he getting set up for a terrible fall, or was Henson just back to his double-dealing ways that usually work out well? At any rate, he had all the necessary paperwork for this morning's proceedings.

By 7am, Monday, Wallace Henson had drawn up a counter lawsuit against Daylight Security just in case it was needed and had negotiated with Bruce to reduce the sell price by the 20 million, and had asked Linda to marry him, so when he arrived at the offices of White, Farmer, and White he felt totally alive.

Cedric White was standing near the elevator to greet the parties as they got off. First, Wallace Henson, then Jake Austin arrived about 9:35, then Randall Brewer and his team came in about 9:45. Bruce and Thomas rode in together and arrived five minutes later. Sally Penfield was already seated in the large conference room, talking on the phone, and taking notes. Ronald White walked in and took a seat next to Sally.

"How's it going kid?" he says to her.

"Not bad. These things always require something extra, private companies. There's always a nighttime deal somewhere that comes to light at the last moment," she says with a slight, knowing grin.

"Yeah," he agrees. "Our boy is a mess, Henson. Anything else?" Ronald asks.

"I expect something. Good thing Brewer has been at this for years as well. We had lunch Saturday, and his guy isn't a 'day camper' either. All this money, and so much bull shit," she reports.

"Wasn't he sick or something?" Ronald asks, genuinely concerned.

"Don't get me started. Brewer says he's fine now; that's all I want to know. Anyway, he had signed all the papers, so Mr. Walker will be handling everything," she gives him.

"Will Mr. Robinson be here?"

"I think so. Excuse me, I need to make one more call and spread everything out here in front of me to hand out to the parties. Oh, by the way, thanks for the note, it was helpful."

"Anything for the team," he says, as he swipes his smart phone to view any recent e-mails.

*

Right at 10:00am the interested parties came into the room and took seats. Wallace Henson, Jake, and an assistant sat on the same side of the table as Sally and Ronald; Thomas, Bruce, and Gerald Allen, their Sales Manager, sat on the other with Mr. Brewer and Vincent Moore.

The highly polished oak credenza at the front of the room had a 12-cup coffee pot, several eight-ounce bottles of water, two carafes of juice and some pastries on a large, silver-plated tray. There were no windows here, but the oil painting of hunting parties, and fall scenery provided a backdrop of comfort. The chairs were desk sized, thickly padded leather, and were evenly spaced around the table, initially. When these type proceedings get going chairs are shuffled about so that the participants can ear talk with each other, as further negotiating was the norm.

After the handshaking, eye winks, and general 'Hey, how are you doing?' was finished, Sally called the meeting to order.

"Good morning all, let's make some money!" she chimed to uproarious laughter. "I think everybody knows everybody, and the doorman frisked each of you I hope; we do have knives for sale if anyone is interested!" Again the laughter but mixed by participation. "Okay, for the record, today is December 19, 2011, and we are here for the sale of Weapons Eye Sync, and associated properties to Henson Technologies, and associated interests. I 'm not sure I know this gentleman?" She points to Gerald Allen.

"Yes, Gerald Allen, Sales Manager." he says, and looks around to all.

"How did you find this crowd?" Sally jokes to minimum laughter. "Okay, that's the extent of my standup routine," she says. Everyone claps in agreement at that prospect.

"Firstly, I have the sales agreement, letters of confidentiality, and security agreements. I'm missing the non-compete, and consulting agreements."

Jake's assistant hands them over for their side, and Bruce hands over the others.

"Anything happen not in the original packets?" she asks.

"Yes," Bruce speaks up. "We reduced the price by 20 million, and there are two exclusive rights issues that have to be addressed," he offers, and hands her the notarized papers: one the price reduction, the other agreements pending with Daylight Security. She looks them over and passes them around for each principal to read and initial, if acceptable. The attorneys had discussed the matters last evening and were in accord, so this was a formality. She taps on her phone keypad and in a few seconds a young, female intern knocks on the door, and comes into the room. She stands by Sally, who gathers the papers and asks, "Anything else before I have these copies made with the changes?"

Everyone looks around, smiles to each other, and nod, "Okay." Sally hands the intern the originals, and she heads out the door. After about fifteen minutes of individual messaging, and small talk by the gathered, she returns, and hands Sally the stack of papers, making sure she has the original document first. Sally passes out copies to each, and the laborious task of paper signing, and fine tuning commence.

It takes about twenty-five minutes for all the signing, and fine tuning, and a small side agreement, not to be a part of the record, but understood. It made Jake a little uncomfortable, but these were big boys, and he still had a lot to learn.

After about ten more minutes, enough time to sort copies for each side, and to formalize the original, with addenda, she announces, "You may kiss the bride!" Everyone stands, shakes hands, the eye winks again, and a 1.4-billion-dollar transfer of ownership had been completed.

Chapter Thirty-Seven

"Everybody has signed on except Dr. Taylor," Wallace says after they turn on to Piedmont, heading south to Monroe, then left into Virginia Highlands and on to Henson's condo building. "Do you want to keep the space at the Mears Building or move everything to Alpharetta?" he asks Jake.

"I like being downtown, and the facilities are set up here," Jake says.

"I agree. Jake, look, great job with the purchase and all, here's a little something for your efforts."

Henson hands him an envelope and Jake had to twist his grasp of the steering wheel to get it.

"Should I open it now?" Jake asks.

"Not now, later."

"Thank you."

"You're very welcome. Also, I need you to write a check to Norris Henderson for $20.2 million dollars this week and mail it to Bruce Walker's residence. Use this check, it's from my money market account," Wallace says to him.

"Is this one of those times?" Jake asks.

"Yes and no. Norris Henderson helped out with the deal and had to 'talk' to Helmut Conover at Daylight; that's all you need to know for now," Wallace tells him.

"Yes sir," Jake responds.

"Okay, Phoenix, when are you going?"

"Two weeks, and I'm taking two trainers. They want 50 units, and may have a lead for us in Los Angeles," Jake reports.

"That's right, okay, good. Thanks Jake."

*

Jake drops Wallace off at his place and calls Marie as he pulls off.

"$2.4 million dollars," he says as soon as she answers. "2.4 million dollars," he repeats.

"What's that darling, did you win the lottery?" she asks, being facetious.

"I did, we did, I mean, I got a bonus for my work on the deal. Hooray! Life is good, I love you, I love our kids, and I love the Lord!"

"Amen brother," she says.

"Okay, I'll calm down in a minute. I'll see you in a few. Oh, I love you!"

"Thanks, drive carefully. I love you too. Great job. See you in a few," she says, smiling to herself, proud of her husband, and the work he does to provide for the family.

*

"Tell me about your friend up the street?" Larry asks his brother, Leroy.

"Bruce?"

"Well, Norris Henderson first."

"Wow. Okay. Bruce is Norris. He's a fed, DEA. He busted me back in the day, and we did a trade. We've talked some lately," Leroy shares.

"Why did you show him the paper?"

"Man, I messed up. He still had a 'body' on me, and he was being jammed by his old boss, Jack Moran, as you know, the guy who wrote the 824 paper," Leroy says.

"I know all that, why didn't you tell me?" Larry asks him.

"Stupid, just stupid. I'd almost forgotten about the body, but he hadn't. You know how bad those boys are, and I didn't want you to become active again," Leroy recounts.

"Okay. Is there anything else, does he have anything else on you?"

"No, that's it, and if it hadn't been for...okay, that's it."

"What's Norris doing?" Larry asks.

"Moving tons of weed."

"But isn't he in witness protection?"

"Fox in the hen house," Leroy answers.

"Didn't they, his neighbor Thomas, didn't they just sell their company for a billion dollars?" Larry asks.

"They did. You know, it's never enough with those guys."

*

"Mr. Klinger, Larry Fleming here, thanks for calling."

"Good to talk to you. Harry thinks a lot of you."

"He tells me you want to come to his last session?" Larry confirms.

"I do want to come. You've worked wonders with him. Look, I've got something to tell him, and I'd like to do it there. It's pretty heavy, and I need to tell him," Mr. Klinger says.

"Okay. Do I need to know ahead of time?"

"Probably."

*

"Jack, I think we can help each other with something," Bruce starts.

"The brothers?" Jack confirms.

"Yeah. I believe they think they're as smart as we are. They may need an old-fashioned lesson?" Bruce asserts.

"I don't want to go that far back, but we do need to protect our interests," Jack responds.

"What do you propose?" Bruce asks.

"A simple knockout," Jack says.

"How about the top guy?" Bruce asks.

"We missed that chance in '08. Plus, he's really helping everybody get what they need, so let him finish. We'll get David elected in '16 and then we'll put them all back in their places!" Jack says gleefully.

"When should we meet?" Bruce asks.

"Soon, and we need our best people on him quick," Jack offers.

"Together?" Bruce asks.

"That may be tough. Leroy first, to get Larry hot, then get him," Jack offers.

"Do you think that'll work?" Bruce asks.

"His wife?" Jack asks.

"Oh hell no! I don't want a full-scale riot here in Atlanta," Bruce says.

"So what's first?" Jack asks.

"Get the 'group' together and schedule the reconnaissance; then move!" Bruce orders.

Chapter Thirty-Eight

Harry and John Klinger arrived for the 4 o'clock appointment on time. Larry was just finishing a call from Mr. Whitlock who informed him that the family was healing and that maybe they could come in soon for a tune-up. Larry told him that would be appropriate, and for him to call back to formalize a time.

"Well, Klinger and Klinger," Larry greeted them.

"Yes we are," spoke Harry as they came in, and shook hands.

"John, Larry; good to meet you. Come on in and have a seat. Over there if you like," Larry said, pointing to the sofa. Harry sat in the armchair near the table desk.

"So, from weed head to new head," Larry joked with Harry.

"It is new; I have to remind myself I'm the same person. This is cool," Harry responds.

"John, what do you think?"

"It is like a new person; same son, new ways." He says. "I can't believe it sometimes."

"Harry, anything we haven't covered that's been on your mind?" Larry asks him.

"No, but Jessica and I really enjoyed reading the story again. That's a cool story. People need to read that story. Man, from back in the 70s; man!" Harry says, enthused. "Kids, I mean, maybe not old people," he adds.

"Okay, good. John, anything?"

John turns to look directly at his son.

"Harry, I know sometimes I didn't raise you right. With your mama gone it was so much I didn't know how to change."

"Dad, you did okay."

"Thanks son. But my race views, they were wrong. I should have changed sooner."

"Why dad, it's okay?"

"Well, I've met someone."

"You've got a girlfriend? Where is she? You haven't told me?"

"Well, it's kind of starting slow. That's why I haven't told you yet. But what I need to tell you is that she's black and white, mixed race I guess they call it. Her father is black, and her mother is white. She's never met them. She was put up for adoption by the mother when she was in college. She doesn't know anything about them."

Harry sits in silence, stunned. Larry looks on, clinically.

"Man, this is blowing my mind. Are y'all the same age?"

"Yeah, but I've got a couple of months on her; we're both 41."

"You were such a hard-core racist! How can you do this?"

"I guess the same way you did this; same man, new ways."

Larry starts to comment but doesn't.

*

John Sheriff, engineer, and black career agent, acting DOD liaison for Commerce, talked to Wallace Henson on two previous occasions about Jack Moran, and how he and Bruce Walker had orchestrated Henson's financial loss back in 2010. John was now overseeing the shutdown of Hobe due to the racial atmosphere in the Midwest, and because of Henson's control of certain semi-conductor and sensor business segments and his advanced recognition devices, there were a few items to clarify. Henson's loss could now be recouped, and the ones responsible brought to justice. The military was having great success with the CR2 units, so Henson's purchase of WES took on greater significance. Wallace didn't take much vindication from what he was hearing, he had overpaid to acquire WES. The racial issues were beyond his grasp as he rarely employed minorities, didn't really know any, and could care less about the crime statistics, except they would help his companies sell units. Even though his one black advisor, Nelson Davis, had recommended a black counselor, he still didn't know if he could, adjust. He was to see this Fleming guy in early January, so he would keep an open mind, "Some of them are quite talented," Henson had offered to himself.

*

Thomas was coming around to the notion that Bruce was double dealing somehow. After debt, and general company overhead was addressed, plus severances and equipment accounting expenses, and corporate and individual tax liabilities, Thomas should net about 400 million, and Bruce about 84 million from the sale of WES.

He felt fortunate that he had left the DEA persona at Hobe, but noticed that Bruce was still a rogue, operating outside the legal bounds of government oversight. Something about the whole German lawsuit they were still fighting was not clean. Maybe Helmut and Bruce were closer than Thomas realized?

Chapter Thirty-Nine

Celia and Mary were having lunch at the Oakhill Grille in Tucker. Celia ordered a Smoked Salmon Caesar Salad, and Mary was having Chicken and Grits, with Texas Toast. Their friendship had developed more the past five years as both had gotten back into art classes of their persuasion, Mary recently taking a class on Enhancing Background for watercolors, and Celia using her smartphone for most of her picture taking.

"The Quentin Resort on SSI, Heather's Jewelry Show in 1990. You were the photographer, remember, you bought one of my watercolors and we exchanged cards, then ran into each other at the Grand Canyon in October, just before they closed for the season," Mary is saying, recounting how they met.

"Oh wow, that's right!" Celia confirms.

"Was that a beautiful color scheme or not?" Mary adds. "We've been twice, once in July, but the fall is the best I think," Mary offers. 'Which leads me to a question if I may?"

"Of course, if I have an answer," Celia gives her.

"How have you and Leroy made it work? I mean, total opposites on so many levels! I'm more than curious, more envy at this stage of life," Mary says to her.

"The race or crime facts?" Celia asks, taken aback by this somewhat odd tidbit for lunchtime conversation.

"I'm just fascinated, that's all, my dear. I certainly don't mean any harm, or to be intrusive. I don't know anyone else I can talk to about this," Mary apologizes.

"I understand, but like most relationships it's complicated, yet we complement each other so well. We just work at it. Oddly, or maybe not, generally, it's still about a guy and a gal. I'm an artist, he's a businessman; sound familiar?" she puts it back to Mary.

"You know, you're right. Bruce and I are the same when you put it that way. But the race stuff, does it come up?" she asks.

"Not like you think. Only as much as the white way has been dominate here in America, I take it for granted and must stay aware that his experience is different. His criminal past happened so early for him, and he blossomed in prison, as it were. Now, he did get into some bad stuff right before we met, and went away again, but he's been awesome the past 13 years we've been together. You know, Yale or Jail, it's what you do with it!" Celia explains.

"You're so healthy about it all. My crowd would be scared to death!" Mary comments.

"We've just not had the overt racial challenges, as it were. My friends all accepted him, and he accepts them, with prejudice." They laugh. "Just like all men seem to do with women," Celia offers.

"I get that," Mary shares.

"When we met, it just happened. I mean, New Mexico, almost in the middle of nowhere, early on a Saturday morning, and he helps with my camera? Hollywood has not done that one yet!" Celia observes and laughs.

"So it's really that simple?" Mary asks.

"If it's love, it's always simple, but hard sometimes."

"How about you and Bruce, he's done some interesting things from what I hear?" Celia observes.

Mary starts to cry, and cry. Finally, after the waiter brings over some tissue, and more tea for both, Mary begins, "I guess that's what I really want to talk about. I'm becoming very afraid that Bruce has become someone I don't like. I've accepted his past, classified work, and we have a great life in so many ways, but I don't think he can turn it off. I don't know if therapy would help, but he's not right. Something very sinister has overtaken his life. I'm not sure he even knows it anymore," Mary shares. "Maybe we can talk more another time?"

"Of course, soon."

*

Security at the State Department had to scan Larry a third time, and still got no reading, so he had to take off all his clothes, have them hand searched, as well as a visual body check by two different officers, a man, and a woman. The installation ceremony for Darlene's cousin, Cary Hollis as an Ambassador was about to start, and The Service could not approve him to come near the president. Larry was comfortable with it all, and didn't stress about it, however, Cary wanted him in there because Larry's grandfather had inspired her to get into Foreign Service, and the Diplomatic Corps. After the lead security agent went over the guest list, and saw Larry's credentials, and the thirty minutes to observe how he carried himself, and that he was from Atlanta, he was allowed in without further scrutiny.

The ceremony was flawless, and the president was generous in his praise of Cary's work in France and Western African capitals. Her acceptance speech was gracious, and she mentioned Larry's grandfather's wisdom, and gentle guidance in family and community matters.

At the evening social, Darlene and Larry enjoyed meeting workers stationed throughout the world as they beamed with pride talking about Cary. Darlene was especially glad she got to meet the first lady, who didn't stay long past a short visit with the new ambassador. The evening was pleasant enough, and they left early to drive around D.C.

*

Thomas and Shirley left their last family conference pleased and relieved. Thomas' recovery was complete, and the neurological tests showed only minimal manifestation of progression, only age-appropriate memory decline. They were making plans to spend the spring and summer in Wisconsin to remodel the farmhouse there.

They would keep the house in Summit Chase for fall and winter, and otherwise travel to places they had been discussing the past five years.

Thomas was glad to be out of the game, and looked forward to minimal commitments, and leisurely hobbies. Shirley was happy to volunteer with the Girl's Club when in town, as time permitted. They both had gotten new smart phones, and fewer people had their new numbers. They were not isolating but were loosening ties from the past.

The hazy light of half a moon,
when morning work has just begun.

They both received packages on April 13, 2012. Jack Moran was not home for the 1pm delivery so he had to go to the post office a mile away to sign for his. He returned home, went to the study, and saw that the package was from San Francisco. He opened it, and a CR2 unit was inside. He pushed the activation switch, and read from the screen, "Time to scan yourself," and in .73 seconds he saw: Weapon-misguided intelligence, Intent-discourage minority progress, Motive- assassinate first black president, Result-The Marshall Service will come for you within the hour.

Bruce was home and received his package from the regular postal delivery person. He saw that the package was from San Francisco and opened it. Inside was a CR2 unit as well. He pushed the activation switch, and read from the screen, "Time to scan yourself," and in .73 seconds he saw: Weapon-murder, Intent-domination of others, Motive-indeterminate, Result-The Marshall Service will come for you within the hour.

*

Larry felt assured of his place, truly he had become a wise and concerned advisor, free of his past indiscretions, free of the excesses of his youth and young adulthood. As he sat outdoors, on the patio, he watched Molly, their three-year old Tabby, glide around the backyard. She had caught her first bird and chipmunk within the past week, and today she was out, watching and chasing as the squirrel was teaching her some lessons about speed and agility. It would jump from the bird feeder, run, then climb back up a tree, run the length of a limb, cross over to another tree, then disappear, as small limbs and branches moved back to a stable position.

He thought of what people said about his mother's father, Big Man, and his example of restraint during the forties and fifties, that a certain carriage was necessary to counter the racism of the day, that smart, mannered black folk could serve by day, and feast by night. That a timeless, dignified way of handling oneself assured success in public, or private places, that you would be protected, if civility were maintained.

Chapter Forty

Rhonda Clemente' was the office administrator for Hudson Graphics. They specialized in designing covers for books. It was a three-person office that had been in business for 35 years. Rhonda came aboard in 2005. She helps run the office, and now creates covers as well. She had worked for a clothing retailer for 12 years, where she hired on right after graduating college. She lives in a modest apartment in east Buckhead, has a cat, Suzy, and has never married. She had one steady, Leon, for about two years, but he met someone else, a guy, and moved on. She has dated off and on, and has a few friends to do things with, but generally not a lot of social activity. She met John at a Hawks game a year ago, and they spend time together. His wife died several years ago, and he has a teenage son, who Rhonda has not met, yet. John and his son, Harry, have had a few issues related to the son's pot use, but he seems fine now, and John was going to a counseling session with him today. John had asked Rhonda if it was okay if he mentioned her as a friend with whom he has feelings for to his son. She said okay, as she has feelings for him as well. They've had a couple of hook-ups, and the relationship has gone to another level, which is scary for them. John had mentioned that at some point they may want to consider counseling. She's in agreement with that.

*

Randall Green worked for the local hardware store on Thurmond St. He was one of the four clerks who had been with Mr. Jones forever. If there were 15,000 items in stock Randall knew what they were, and where they were located. Basically his brain had a map of the 2,400-square foot space. If he had touched it, or moved it, or if someone else had moved it, and he had passed by it more than three times he could tell you whether it was old, new, or had been re-packaged as a returned item. He could recite prices, tax amounts, and warranties, if any, before you got to the register to pay, or were in the back trying to make sense of a specification. Also, if anyone brought up the tune memory game you'd want him on your side. Popular songs starting from when he was age nine to now, Randall would probably have a 94% success rate. It was always entertaining when someone new would challenge him, and an obscure piece would be played, to watch Randall wink, and sit back as the other person strained his or her memory before Randall would comfortably name it, as if it should be common knowledge. Fortunately, he had a good spirit about it all, and people loved to spend time with him.

*

Linda was getting good with the notion that no further action was going to happen on the marriage proposal. It had come on the heels of two fabulous weekends of lovemaking and togetherness that both desperately needed. Linda was able to feel like a woman again, and not just the hired help. A month had passed, and because the offices were so spread out she only saw him pass by once, after a staff meeting to christen the company's new home. She wasn't sure if he drank some of the champagne, and he did not try to avoid her, though they did not make a path to each other. She chalked it up to experience and settled back into the work they pay her to do, and if he needs her again he would certainly call, like the drunk that he is. Sober, they had a great time, but she knew that the alcohol was his true love.

*

Helmut Conover was angry about the legal judgements as he did not get the $6.4 million bonus Bruce Walker had promised, nor the exclusive rights for the skin color recognition sensors. He had been outplayed, and now that Bruce was in jail, and Thomas had moved away somewhere, he would go after Wallace Henson, the new owner of WES. He had not thought Mr. Henson so crafty, but the embarrassment he endured from losing the court case was causing him to plan an unfortunate accident for the gentleman once he completed the sale of his own company.

*

Wallace and Jake were putting in 12-hour days working on the restructuring. Even though Wallace had Jake by 20 years it was usually the junior man calling time out at the end of the day. Henson always operated at a high energy level but seemed particularly focused and energized now. Staff was in place, and there was not much to remodel. They did add a sterile chip manufacturing machine, and had the clean room re-designed by an applied technology firm. Jake was glad Henson Technologies was flush with cash and decided to pay certain expenditures up front, not on time payments. Henson had told him about a stash of 500 pounds of gold he bought at $267.00 per ounce that now traded at $1,768.00 per ounce. The only area of immediate concern had been Daylight Security, but Sally assured them the lower court ruling would stand.

Wallace Henson was on that high that only conquest knows, another deal, another rung up the ladder. His long hours and hard work had paid off again, and now he was conversing in the billion-dollar range. It all had fit so well, his loyal staff of 32 was still around, and Jake was proving to be the right man for the CEO slot. He could seek new ventures, or travel the world, he could slow down, write a how to book about his steady climb to wealth. He could volunteer some time, and surely pursue some avenues to give back, as it were, to certain charities. Oddly, he had the 'look at me now bravado' towards his ex-wife, a woman he had not seen in over twenty years. He felt with this level of accomplishment, surely, he could have one drink of the champagne that was left from the celebration. But, he had come to accept that booze was no longer his friend, and that he probably was an alcoholic, and like he had been told, even one is too much for him. He knew, also, that at some point he would need to call Linda and apologize for his exuberance and tell her that he enjoyed their time together sober, but he just wasn't in a place to commit to a definite relationship of that nature. He thought he would tell her that he was coming from a place of gratitude for her services, and he got a little carried away, he didn't know how to just say 'Thanks.'

Chapter Forty-One

Jake was spending more time with the research people and getting used to the technical aspects of why they should consider buying certain small companies that had already designed, developed, and fabricated the next generation of sensors. He could speak of the MEMS based sensing devices for gyros and accelerometers, and how that may lead to some business in the automotive industry. Or, as he was expecting his people to come up with, new ways to help people understand people by using a variation of the CR2 units. He wanted to exploit the peace and harmony abundant in the world and have Triple Line System become the real peace maker. Could a device help law enforcement change a split-second decision about whether a suspect is lunging forward with purpose, or simply losing coordination due to the stress of his crises? Or better understand the spatial ratios of when to disarm someone, six feet, ten feet? He had the vision, and resources, but the scientist would have to prove or disprove the potential for effectiveness. All this thinking was close to what WES and Henson Tech had done, but he wanted the new devices to help the world in a different way, and not just by chasing down the bad guys. He wanted to make it safer for the afflicted, who were in crisis, and whose actions and movements were harder to discern. Hopefully, there's a chip for that!

*

Linda called Jake to ask for a few moments of his time. He said he could see her at 11:30 this morning.

Walking down the long hall, and walking up the one flight of stairs she still wasn't sure if she needed to resign, or ask for some time off? Her department was not full-time, really, as the people who worked here were generally very healthy, and rarely came to the clinic to have vitals checked, or to discuss health care policy changes. Jake's assistant escorted her to the office, and he stood at the door to greet her. "Linda, how are you, come on in?" he says to her.

Jake's office was full sized, with a comfortable glass topped desk, and mesh back chairs. His conference table could seat six, and had enough space to spread papers, books, and charts to be passed around and viewed by several people at a time as they leaned forward, and moved around, after pushing chairs out of the way.

The credenza had pictures of the family, a few books, and a bronze figure of a horse at full gallop sitting on the top. On the shelves, behind the closed doors was an assortment of necessities for entertaining guests when there was a need, small plates, plastic eat ware and cups, soda, small bottles of water, and a half pint bottle of Bourbon. Of course Jake didn't drink, but on occasion a prospect might need to be loosened up a bit. The other furnishings were modest, with the only extravagance an oil painting of a valley in eastern Kentucky with an older woman instructing or admonishing some kids in front of a mountain cabin, a short stick in her hand serving as a pointer, for emphasis; she and the kids clothed in tattered woolens. The soft lighting over it helped produce a mystical, dream-like quality to the scene. It was signed and dated May 10, 1789, by Lonnie White.

"Let's sit over here," he suggested, guiding her to an armchair that faced into the office, as he rolls his desk chair from behind the desk, and came closer to her. She tries to smile, and Jake senses this could be a difficult conversation.

She was dressed in pleated slacks, a white, plain blouse, and a Blazer. She wore medical smocks most of the time, but wanted to have a different, professional look today. Her hair was brushed and shiny, her facial skin was healthy looking, tight, with few wrinkles, and her weight seemed appropriate for her skeletal frame. She worked out twice a week with light weights, and old school exercises and short jogs around the track at the YWCA near her home.

She recently had a financial check-up and had a plus balance of $490 thousand dollars, her house and car were paid for, and little debt elsewhere. She co-owned a condo with her brother that produced about 18 thousand dollars of income for her per year. If she took some time off, she had enough to live on for a while. And if she stayed on, she would ask Jake what would be her new role? She knew she would have to bring up Wallace, yet she wasn't sure how much to share, and what questions to ask Jake about that whole deal? Wallace had been good for her in a lot of ways, and she surely did not want to trash him, or jeopardize her future with the company, if she decided to stay. She kind of wanted to stick around, but she was becoming more uncomfortable, especially now that Wallace was staying sober, and really didn't need her anymore. They both adjusted to a more comfortable position, then Linda began to speak.

"Thanks for seeing me, Mr. Austin," she starts. "I don't want to waste time, so I'll get right to it. I need some clarity as to my job here moving forward. My nursing duties are minimal, and the reports I present to staff are not crucial. Most of the people here are very healthy in mind, body, and spirit, and the health insurers send out individualized screening updates. My role is part time at best, so I was wondering if now is when I should take a sabbatical and see what my needs are," she offers.

"Ms. Mitchell, thanks for coming up. I've wondered when we would have this conversation. I know you've had a, shall we say, special relationship with Mr. Henson. I'm sure it hasn't been easy. So, tell me what's going on?" he asks.

"Honestly, I'm not sure. Should rules of confidentiality apply here?" she questions, more to herself than for Mr. Austin.

"We probably need to be honest, discrete, but truthful at this time," he leads.

"You're right, no secrets necessary," she adds.

"He has told me, in a general way, how helpful you have been to him over the years, personally, and thus to the company. I think he would approve of you coming to see me."

"I think so. How much history should I give you?" she asks.

Jake fights back an urge to look at his watch, then says, "Take your time. It's important that you make the right choices, now, and going forward," he says with as much compassion as he can give in this setting.

"Let's see if I can keep it brief; I came on about 15 years ago as a clerk in accounting, and being a young, single female, and having a financial short fall when I went to nursing school, I accepted an offer of financial help from him. There were no strings, and I offered to pay it back. As I started using my nursing training here more, and as he started getting in trouble with the alcohol we became more dependent on each other, and sleeping together, occasionally, well not that, on occasion. I sort of went into a strange place with it as I rarely dated anyone else, and he was busy all the time with running the businesses. He never feigned affection, and I didn't push for it, though a girl hopes, sometimes. So as the years have moved on I've sat around, waiting, hoping that something bigger would happen between us. Well, before the purchase of the other business, two weeks before, we were in Miami, acting like tourist and lovers. I mean it was everything I had hoped for, he was sober, I felt a part of him, and he was attentive, and acted like a husband. Then we came back to his condo, and continued with wonderful meals, nights out and about, and great lovemaking. Early Sunday morning, about four hours before he got dressed to meet you at the lawyers' office he asked me to marry him, but he hasn't said a word since, even, I don't know, avoiding me at the office celebration last Thursday. I just can't bare it!" She becomes tearful, and looks about the office, focusing for a moment on the old woman's stern posture in the painting. "So, that's why I think I should leave for a time or look to move on somewhere else."

Jake feels stumped by her dilemma, and doesn't want to offer an easy answer, or give too much feedback, he thinks they call it.

"Jake, sir, I'm not asking you to speak to him, I'm just trying to ascertain my best course for the short term," she gives him.

"We have some exciting options coming up, you'll have a job to do here. Take some time, go by your office when we finish, get what you need, let Clarice, my assistant, know whatever you need to pass on, and take two months off, with pay. Update us, or not, but come back then, and see what's up. If you find something else, take it. Do what seems best for you. If I may, you're 47, do your thing! I'll have Clarice write up the agreement, and you take off, okay?"

"I'll do it! Thank you, sir," she says, leaving his office and planning never to return.

Chapter Forty-Two

Mary decided to divorce Bruce, and she agreed to have the fund raiser at her home before packing up and moving back to St. Simons. It all went down so fast, and she felt bad, knowing Bruce had made a lot of what he termed strategic choices that were really just wrong. He had grown up with a tough, privileged crowd who were used to doing over the top things for the good of their friends, but the ethical component was lacking. She was sad for him, and sad for herself, but she held on to, 'such is life.'

Celia was helping to get the house ready, and the protection detail had made special precautions that would be put in place two days before the event. The Summit Chase Homeowners Association Board would convene a special meeting to coordinate the six hours of lockdown for the residents. Security had done the research, and the only issue would be with Bob Turner who was dying of AIDS at home. His sister was his care giver, and medical procedures would be in place should a crisis develop. Also, Ernie Weston, the 98-year-old physician hoped he could meet the man but understood the logistics. It would be a highlight of his long life to meet the first African American president. Fortunately, POTUS agreed to come early and spend time with the distinguished doctor. Otherwise, security was routine as most of the residents were retired and didn't need to move around too often; a six-hour stay in the house was not a hardship. Celia and Leroy had decided to return to New Mexico to live and would be looking again at a house about a mile away from Darla, Darlene's friend. They would fly out the morning after the event.

Larry and Darlene had little to prepare, or change, as the plan was for them to come over, greet a few guests, then leave. They'd had their moment with the Elites in D.C at Cary's installation service.

*

The assassins who had been called off in 2008 had been re-activated. The exact timing would be finalized a day before, but now they were practicing on a replica home. It was in a field near David Turner's house, but the 2016 candidate, nor any of his people knew of the planning. Jack Moran had left specific plans months before he was hauled off to the Federal Penitentiary in Alabama, and word was going around the yard that Bruce Walker had been transferred to the super max facility after it was discovered he had been involved in the brutal lynching of six members of the Mayfair family of Tennessee. Something about eight tons of marijuana that had been misplaced.

The missing piece was still Larry Fleming, and they had determined he would be eliminated this time for his mistake in 1973. The 824 paper he found had little meaning now, but he was the only person alive who saw them all in one place; "If only he had not survived!" they had said.

*

What Larry remembered was the flash, then the pop, as he crawled the sixty-five feet away from the farmhouse. Sixteen men had been lost, and he had to complete the mission. His physical symptoms were starting, and he would need to dose in twenty minutes. He sensed the weakness in his stomach, but his focus was the same, "shoot the dope, then take out the cancer." His gear pack was heavier because he retrieved Sullivan's that contained the explosives. He was to leave it on the right side of the building, then put the switch under the fourth planter, beside the wall. He was sad the men were killed when he left his post to go cop dope, but guilt would not help him now; the dope would. For what those guys had done to those black soldiers, they could not stay on earth, and Larry was not going to fail.

He placed the packages, dosed on the spot, then crawled away. He activated the switch, and the payload finished the 16 offenders. He started his nod, and 15 minutes later he scurried away, unnoticed. After visits to St. Peter's and The Sistine Chapel, he returned to his duty station in B.K., with little memory of what he had accomplished.

*

Helmut Conover flew into Hartsfield-Jackson Atlanta International Airport at 5:27pm on July 19. He drove the 115 miles north to Lake Hartwell to meet with Wallace Henson who expected him about 8:30pm. Wallace hoped they could resolve their issues, but Helmut had other plans. He was enraged about the double cross, and the millions he lost, plus losing control of the firm he founded and nurtured for 30 years.

"Yes, who is it?" Wallace had asked as he'd gone to the door and opened it before he heard the response. Helmut knocked him back, then tripped him to the floor, and beat him about the head and shoulders. Wallace struggled to push him up, then off him. The killer rebounded, backhanded him, then bowled him over flat to the floor. Wallace scrambled, pushed a sofa a few feet, bumped his head on a glass topped mahogany coffee table, and noticed he felt out of breath. Helmut paused, lunged at him, missed, and Wallace rolled around to the killer's back and hit him in the head, twice, as hard as he could, then Helmut swung around and was on him with the knife drawn.

He plunged it into Wallace's chest, hitting a rib and withdrew it, then, with all his power jammed the 4-inch blade deep into his neck, tearing muscle, arteries, and skin. The assailant jumped back as Wallace clutched his neck trying to stop the flow of blood, but it was over. He shimmied violently, fell to the floor, rolled over a time, yet he was able to crawl out the side door to the back deck, look up at Helmut, who followed him, as blood pooled on the wood flooring. Helmut then took out a pistol and shot him in the head.

Chapter Forty-Three

The neighborhood was abuzz about the event at Mary's house tonight. Most had never met her, or even had occasion to wave, and certainly didn't know about Bruce. The speculation game was in full play as friends called each other and tried to find out who was invited from the community, and what big-name politicians and business leaders would be there. Atlanta now had a lot of top-quality leaders in both areas, so the mix of North and South should be comfortable.

Security could be heard and seen setting up barriers about 7:00am, and the few residents who ventured out during the day could not bring anyone else back in as identification, and car checks would be thorough. A position in the woods formed a horseshoe thirty yards deep for the perimeter, and guards had thoroughly searched there the previous two weeks. Mary's house, of course, was already a fortress with ten agents patrolling the ¾ acre site continually, in and outside, for the 8pm start time of the event. The featured guests would arrive about 8:30.

The Fleming's house was secure as well because Leroy and Celia stayed over, and Celia had become Mary's main helper. Security had learned from the previous high-level guest that a line from Larry's house, back through the woods, and onto the interstate could be a problem. A cement barrier, 80 feet long, and ten feet high had been left in place, and would be stationed by three guards. Based on a house burglary seven months ago, security found a weak spot left of the main entry point and closed that off with a retractable metal gate that would have three guards as well. It wasn't clear to anyone in place whether 'Dunkirk' would enter by car, or helicopter, because that would be determined later in the day. The airport was 16 miles away, south, around I-285. Either mode of transport would be convenient at those times, coming in, or leaving out.

*

The assassins hadn't planned to get them in one place at the same time. POTUS was a bonus now, but Larry was the main target. They found out which house, and the approximate time of the event at 10:45am when one of the team's sisters finished sexing one of the guards over near the high school. The team was made up of 10 guys and two women, highly trained and skilled. Each had combat experience from at least one, and possibly three of the larger conflicts throughout the world the past seven years. They were well paid and ruthless, and all had some injury from war or training.

The team split up, then arrived at 7:45pm. At the first entry point they encountered mock-ups of several policemen. The second point had the same, with four mock-ups of security agents. When the two teams cautiously arrived at Mary's house there were cardboard images of Larry, POTUS, and Rita. They were dumb founded. The Service Agents came up, arrested them, and took them to a federal holding facility nearby.

Rita was laughing as she sipped coffee and handed POTUS the check for $2.57 million dollars. The fund raiser had been a success, and it was all handled online. Larry sat comfortably in his living room enjoying his guests and watching the new dream unfold.

EPILOGUE

Leroy was running through the woods behind his house. The DEA Agents had stopped just before crossing onto his property. The gunshots they fired missed him, and they never heard Larry come up behind them. He was quick and certain, and they fell on the spot, just short of the county line. He called 911 and reported the scene he had discovered. The ambulance arrived twenty minutes later. Larry was not waiting for them.

*

Leroy and Larry Fleming had officially retired from active duty, as it were. After completing the last investment ventures with Jake Austin Leroy no longer had the drive or energy to advise on or research present day business opportunities. It was all esoteric and too new age for him to sharpen his old-time skills. Like his uncles he was too much of a gentleman to practice the edges necessary for today's financial programs. Even though he returned to prison for a short stint in his early forties.

Larry, as well, knew he was not as quick as he used to be, mentally nor physically. He had recounted enough stories from the drug days that he could no longer be helpful to clients. At 69 and 70 years of age they were tired of the street world they knew whether it was played in a conference room or on MLK Jr. Drive. They were learning how to sit on the porch and discuss events of the day with a best friend. They were no longer needed on the battlefield.

Celia, Leroy's wife, continued to paint and instruct a few students in the studio out back of the house. There had not been much travel the past year and they were quite content at 615 Arlington Circle with its stunning view of the open marshland, lake, and abundant oaks and pines sprinkled about. Celia had produced several versions in watercolor and acrylics and the ones she hadn't sold were hung in the studio as testimony to her craft and the beauty of the scenery before them. Larry, for his part, had come over and penned several poems to capture the essence of the magical oasis she so wonderfully represented, and Leroy had extended the patio and outdoors room to accommodate guests who marveled at the evening light as it in the tops and mid sections of the trees. One didn't need to finish a cocktail to become relaxed in this setting.

*

"Excuse me," the woman pardoned as she asked, "Are you Larry Fleming?"

"Yes, I am," he answered, "And you are?"

"Stephanie Griffin. I did some work for your brother Leroy a few years ago when he worked with Cynthia Tucker out in San Francisco; H.U.N."

"Yes, and your role?" he asks.

"I'm an attorney."

"Well, I won't hold that against you," he offered as an ice breaker. "How did you recognize me?" he asks.

"Jake and Marie Austin's house in Pennsylvania, their 20th wedding anniversary, shortly after the death of your wife. We spoke about that."

"Oh yes, I do remember now. We talked of my work, and you had just lost a son to addiction. Two injured souls at the time."

"Yes, but I remember it was a pleasant affair and you were a gentleman," she says to him.

"Yes, it was. Do you live near here?" he asks.

"I just moved back from California; I bought a place just behind the building here, in Redfern Village. I bought one of the first condominiums."

"Nice. I'm back up the hill on Romaine Street."

"Oh, the big houses?"

"No, I'm not one of those. I have a smaller older one that I've remodeled."

"I looked up there and decided I didn't need that much space."

"Good for you."

"So, what's a guy like you doing in a place like this?"

"Veggie run, plus some meats to freeze for the next few weeks."

"So, when will you have me over so I can see how the other half lives?" she says in jest.

"Friday; but that's after you show me the condo life."

"I'm a burger and fries girl. Tomorrow?"

"Sure, that's good, I can do burgers about once a month," he says.

"Okay, good, about six?"

"I'll be there. Unit number?"

"1506. The concierge will see you in. Have your ID ready," she warns with laughter.

"I will; I'll get a new one made today!" To which they both laugh heartily.

Chapter 2

Before going to prison Leroy ran with a rough crowd. They attended high school classes infrequently, bothered the girls when they attended, and showed off their intellects when given a chance, although briefly and with stage presence. It was a separation, not a collaboration. Leroy didn't know he was a leader but when he was busted by the feds there was a long list of violations upon decency and good order. A fifteen-year-old should not have been exposed to so much corruption so early in life. But Leroy loved the streets.

Jake Austin, on the other hand, was about as strait laced as they come, good student, good civilian, good young man. He was responsible, aware, and genial. He learned all that from his father who was a general clerk at the county courthouse before going back to school to get his law degree. He had maintained a small but prosperous real estate firm for forty years.

Jake and Marie Tolliver knew each other from high school but only dated after college and married within a year. They had three children two years apart as Jake set about his business career working as a manager in a manufacturing plant. He did well and went back to school at twenty-seven, completed a master's degree in business administration, and rose to VP of Operations.

He met Wallace Henson at a conference on Linear Programming as Henson was one of the presenters. Jake was impressed with the presentation and his ideas about using decision mathematics to establish production flow charts.

Oddly, Mr. Henson approached Jake after his lecture.

"I hear from my sources that you are familiar with silicon chip process and micro-processors," Wallace says surprising Jake early in their conversation.

"I've been at it a few years. I'm not an engineer though," Jake responds.

"I know plenty of them. I'm in need of someone to watch over my expanding business ventures," Mr. Henson offers. "Are you comfortable where you are or are you ready for new challenges?"

"I'm comfortable, but change can be good. What are you offering?" Jake asks, wary as he'd heard rumors about Henson's personal instability.

"I'm not that old but I can use some fresher eyes at the steering wheel as we're about to launch some new products."

"That's exciting!"

"How about if I get some information to you so you can see if you would be interested in joining us?"

"Sure, let me take a look," Jake answers."

"I'll send you an email with some non-proprietary projections as to where I think the industry is heading, and what we're looking at."

"Okay, sounds good."

"More than that, it is good! I'll be in touch."

"Okay. Good talking to you."

*

"Counselor, it's Rita. How are you this morning?"

"Not quite awake," he answers the phone.

"I hear you've retired. Have you given up on the new dream?"

"I thought I completed my work. I don't understand where the younger folks are now. Shouldn't someone else pick up the mantle?"

"You still have work to do. Post some more poems," she tells him.

"Okay," he said as Rita hung up.

*

"Double hearts swell when past sculptures tell
a false regard for human passion
minus the joy of love.

Blue hearts must cover a broken vein of red
coming back to freedom's will
respecting all who care."

*

Rita's cancer had spread, and she was given no more than six months
to live by her doctors. She had remained in good spirits during the
last round of chemical therapy but last week decided to stop further
attempts to prolong her life. She was fulfilled with a sense of freedom
reaching out to the counselor one last time. She had a will drafted to
turn her property over to him, and he could do whatever he wanted to
with it. The house and land were now valued at $1.3 million dollars,
and she had no surviving relatives. She appreciated the counselor
fostering her notions of a new dream and they had accomplished much.
He was a good counselor and friend to his clients and that was what
the new dream was all about, helping those less fortunate. She had been
struck by the fact that he had not treated her as some defective person
speaking out of her mind when they reconnected, he treated her wishes
with dignity and respect. She knew, however, there was one more task
to complete, and Leroy would be involved.

Chapter 3

One could never say that Leroy was naive, or that his scars were as deep as Larry's, but he had played around with some dark characters who were low down and dirty. He was loyal to a fault, yet knew how to trade favor for favor, especially in the drug game. His involvement with the DEA fellows, Bruce Walker, and his partner, was about making some serious cash, but also about keeping an old friend out of prison. Frankie D. had taken a lesser charge years ago to protect Leroy and Larry from some gang activity, but he was a bad boy and was the guy who had molested Rita. Leroy was unaware of that connection and that justice would be served before she died.

*

Stephanie's condominium building was made of repurposed brick from a demolished housing project. Along with the bricks the builder had bought several Italianate window treatments from a junk dealer like ones used on four houses that were built by millionaire families on Jekyll Island back in 1906 as vacation homes. Her unit was spacious at 1,658 sq. ft. upstairs with three bedrooms and two baths with a half bath downstairs near a storage closet. Her decorating pattern was modern with leather, and stainless steel with glass furnishings, but enough wooden bookshelves and accent tables to tone down the sterile, space age look.

She was excited and looked forward to having Mr. Fleming over for dinner, and she had already done general food preparations. She remembered him as being a moody type with brief responses in conversation, yet intelligent and discreet. She was glad he was older and didn't anticipate any awkward sexual moments. He didn't have any flowers, wine bottle, or small package gift wrapped in his hands as he walked down the hill at precisely five-fifty-five. He tapped on the front door with a knuckle and rang the doorbell when he reached her front porch and smiled easily when she opened the door.

"Mr. Fleming, I presume?" she greets him.

"Ms. Griffin, Mr. Fleming has arrived!" he answered as she gestured for him to come in.

"I see you travel light," she said with a laugh.

"I started to bring a small token of my appreciation, but I didn't know if you drank alcohol or were allergic to certain flowers."

"Considerate. You look well."

"Indeed, so do you."

"Well, have a seat, and let's see who is awkward first," she says in jest.

"My lady, you may have the honor," spoken as he swings his arm in a circular fashion in front of him.

"Thank you, kind sir. Let's go sit in the living room as if my father would be making an appearance to look you over," she offers.

"Good, I have no motive except to chew the burger slowly and enjoy our conversation."

"Well played my boy, would you like something to drink?"

"I would but you would have to call the cops at midnight."

"Maintaining your sobriety?"

"Yes, so mineral water will suffice."

"I thought this was going to be a tough evening, but this is good. You give as good as you get."

"Yes, and you have not even shown me the bedroom."

"I don't have one, they're all workspaces!"

"Oh, you're good. What area of law?"

"Plain old criminal defense so don't try to bribe me."

"On second thought I'll defer the tour; why did you invite me over, anyway?"

"I read one of your books and I have questions? I don't think you are a fiction writer. I think you write docudramas."

"Well, let's eat and I'll tell you all about my process."

"Real or fiction?"

"I'm not sure, but let's talk."

Chapter 4

Rita was not feeling well, and didn't know what to do with her feelings about Frankie D. He had harmed her in the worst way, but she had survived. She had told no one about the incident, and her parents had to go with the fact that she started calling herself Rita Bishop, that Rita Owens had died, starting in sixth grade following that afternoon she went missing. It was perplexing and her father had spent the better part of a month questioning kids in the neighborhood if they had seen, or knew anything about her disappearance that afternoon, but he got no answers. That new, haunting, straight ahead blank stare she developed afterwards was heart breaking, but everyone moved on, and she finished elementary and high school with no other problems.

It was only when she turned nineteen that people started describing her behavior as bizarre; she had never had a boyfriend, she was not able to hold a job, she would overdress for the seasons, and she walked around talking to herself. Occasionally she would hold a conversation with someone, but her range of knowledge and articulation was beyond most. Law, religion, philosophical inquiry, or historical facts and figures seemed to spew from her with a level of accuracy and depth that was considered special. Oddly, most of the time she would babble nonsense to the clouds. She was cared for however, and people made way to allow her to move about the small neighborhood of Dexter Village.

Rita had only seen Frankie once in the fifty-nine years since he molested her so seeing him last week stirred up feelings of anger about what he robbed her of. She was not cognizant of what it meant at the time, but she knew she had something to discuss with the counselor the next time she walked up on him.

*

Franklin Delaney was a year older than Rita and performed three other instances of sexual molestation before he turned fourteen, two other young girls and one effeminate young boy. As he started getting into trouble with the law and wound up in juvenile detention, he began to experience confusion about his own sexuality and had to use extreme discipline and fear not to act on certain urges. He began to get into fights and otherwise turned to violence to curb those dominant feelings. He had counseling while inside but was not able to develop a healthy sense of self and turned to drugs and alcohol when he got out. He spent time wandering the streets and at twenty was charged with attempted murder and sentenced to fifteen years in prison. He met Leroy at the state prison in Gainesville.

*

Leroy was tired of the brash new inmate talking loudly and taking advantage of the lesser endowed boys. During one particularly harsh screaming at, and punch to the face of a skinny kid Leroy rushed him from behind, grabbed his shoulders, and challenged him to a real fight. Frankie was surprised and before he could react Leroy slapped his face and threw him down to the floor, continuing to punch him until some other guys broke it up before the guards came in and placed the unit on lockdown.

"Who you dude?" Frankie asked. "Don't touch me again!" he shouted.

"Punk, don't you ever touch another soul in here unless you see me first, or I'll kick your ass some more! Punk!"

Frankie backed away but vowed to himself to do something to Leroy soon. He got his chance an hour later and Leroy was ready with a knife and a broom handle and beat Frankie about the head such that blood spewed forth and the guards and medic had to be called in. They attended his wounds but had to transfer him to a medical facility to control swelling and a large hematoma that developed on the side of his neck. Frankie passed out in the ambulance and CPR had to be performed to get him stable.

Chapter 5

Jake Austin continued to have medical issues related to the stabbing back in 2016. Though the liver and abdominal tissues had healed he had vision and memory lapses that were concerning. He decided to share his difficulties with Marie who was already aware of his struggles.

"I was wondering when you were going to get honest with me?" she said as they sat on the back deck looking out to the mountains of North Georgia.

"I didn't want to believe it was taking me down as much as it was. I need to see the doctors as soon as possible."

"Yes, we do, here's my phone, let's call right now."

*

Another matter important to Jake was that he still had access to over five-hundred pounds of gold bars that Wallace Henson had hidden as a reserve for Henson Technologies from its earliest days of incorporation. At today's price of $1,986 an ounce that would be worth a little over $15,888,000.00. Not a huge amount but enough that he thought he would call Leroy and discuss what to do with this bounty.

*

It had been a hot, rainy July and plants, flowers, and trees were lush and overgrown in the area just past the back wire fence of their home. The remains of the large, old, fallen oak tree provided a resting spot for hawks and smaller birds who happened by, and neither Leroy nor his yard man wanted to disrupt the natural order of things because you still had a wonderful view of the meadow as it stretched three hundred yards southeast past the lake on the left.

Leroy, Celia, Larry, and Stephanie sat around the den discussing events of the day when Larry introduced the concept of time and what had occurred in their lives the past seven years. Of course, Larry and Stephanie had major grief issues as part of their individual stories and had only been seeing each other a few months. Celia and Leroy didn't have much outside of Leroy's business affairs and her painting and teaching; mundane or so they thought.

"You don't play around, do you?" Stephanie spoke up.

"It's just since I heard about the death of an old friend yesterday this whole life journey thing was given new meaning," Larry answered.

"Who?" Leroy asked.

"Marie Thomas, she was ninety. Did you ever meet her? Anyway, we worked together for years and had a social connection that was special as well. She would say I was born too late, that I reminded her of the 'Rat Pack' guys. That I had a swing and swagger that was appealing. She was from New Jersey and partied in New York, Vegas, and L.A. back in the fifties and sixties."

"And who did she say you reminded her of?" Celia asked.

"She never said, just that I was a cool, hip, sophisticated kind of guy. But that was a long time ago."

"You can be entertaining and fun loving," Stephanie chimed in. "What about the recent past though?"

"I'm not sure yet. It's been good times, but different challenges. The nature of my work changed a lot. The issues became tougher, and more dangerous. Clients were older and taking more risks; not fewer. These were people who knew how to be bad," Larry shared.

"This is at the federal level, right?" Celia asked.

"Yes," he answered. "But how about your work?" he asks Celia.

"Well, I think you're right, what I was painting years ago, and how I taught my students was different then; now there seems to be a need for edginess to evoke a kind of passion. I guess it's perspective, experiences, meanings. The world has changed so much. Of course, I don't have the same goals either," she referenced.

"Stephanie?" Celia gestures her way.

"I agree. I'm coming up on sixty and how I did what I did then seems miraculous looking back a decade ago. The cases, the workload, the energy, the consultations, I can't do all that now because of the complexities, legal and social. The definitions have changed, even though I'm still productive. What I retain about the cases has become different; I don't know what kind of results to expect. The state, as it were, may befriend my client without my knowing because they want a better deal than I was offering."

"Being run over?" Leroy asks.

"Yes, and not even being able to ride in the first place sometimes. Victimhood is so much more sophisticated now."

"How do you mean?" Leroy asked.

"Client to Judge: "Your honor, legal marijuana hurt my business, so I had to start dealing heroin, which was more profitable anyway." And the judge says, 'I understand,' and gives him a reduced sentence. And I had to accept it."

"More political?" Celia asks.

"More than you want to know. It's as if they want to kill off a certain segment of society."

"This is huge; let's revisit this?" Larry says.

"Sorry, back to your friend," Stephanie offers.

"Well, she was a classy lady, and when I first met her, I knew we would be friends, now this goes back thirty years. But something about the way we knew each other, I mean we didn't spend a lot of time together, but it was intimate."

"What do you think accounts for that?" Leroy asks.

"I think it was a combination of mother, sister, and some street allure. She was sophisticated for sure, but she had something else, a hidden depth, worldly in a civilized way, with no ill will towards anyone. We just talked, and laughed, and enjoyed good meals together."

"So, I suppose you both had depths unspoken to each other, but somehow perceived?"

"I think that's it, a knowing."

"Did Darlene know her?" Celia asks.

"She met her once I think; she knew I had this older, female friend who I met for lunch on occasion. Nothing more."

"You're pretty lucky," Stephanie spoke up. "Maybe I sense that in you as well, an unspoken depth."

"I think as we get older, we know right away who rode the bus, and who drove to school!"

Chapter 6

"Hey Leroy, It's Jake."

"Hey Jake, what's going on my man?"

"A couple of things. Got a few minutes?"

"For you, extra."

"Good. Leroy, I have not been feeling well and I had the doctors run some tests and do some evaluations related to my memory, and some physical stuff from the incident back in 2016. Hopefully, nothing too much but Marie said she'd noticed some changes in my behavior as well."

"How about right now?"

"I know I'm not a hundred percent, that's for sure, and have not been for some years, you know that. Yeah, but lately I know something is not right."

"Well, you're doing the right thing."

"Yeah, I'll keep you posted. There is one other thing, I found, or rather I remembered that Mr. Henson had given me access to some gold bars he bought while building the business. It's about fifteen million worth, and I'm not sure what to do with it."

"That's a good problem to have."

"Any thoughts?"

"I'm not sure, charity, share with his first employees like we did after the closure of the company?"

"I don't know. I've got to get with legal consul to see if there's any tax or corporate exposure to me. I guess the cache is about ten years old. It predates my hiring on."

"Let me think about it, talk to Larry and some other folks, and see what I come up with. Oh, when will you know something about your tests?"

"In about a week."

"Okay, we'll talk before then."

"Good."

*

Rita had been seen walking about the neighborhood, babbling to herself and having nonsensical interactions with people. She was taken in about a month ago for an evaluation at Avery Mental Institute and listed Larry Fleming as a contact. When they called him, he obliged and went in for a progress conference.

It had been three years since Larry had been inside the building. He had both bad and good memories from his time working there and felt unsteady about Rita's plight. It had been over a year since she contacted him, and they had a fabulous, clear conversation. She had implored him to continue to address the new dream and she was glad to talk to him again.

He entered the lobby and was greeted warmly by the receptionist who had worked the desk for fourteen years and knew of his contributions to the clinical setting. She was dressed comfortably with a crème-colored blouse, knit slacks and black flats. Not much makeup and a pair of gold earrings adorned her peach hued ear lobes. She was direct and professional.

"Yes, how may I help you, Mr. Fleming? Good to see you again."

"Thank you, Florence," he responded, not needing to read the name plate in front of her. "Good to see you as well. I'm here for a case Conference at two with Lindsey Baker, a social worker."

"Yes, she was just up here checking to see if you had arrived. I'll call her."

Within a few moments Ms. Baker was pushing open one of the electronically locked doors and signaled for him to come in. As he passed through, he heard the loud click of the large magnets being reconnected. Oddly, it put a smile on Larry's face.

He and Ms. Baker were not familiar, but she had been filled in by staff as to the eminence of Mr. Fleming and was told not to feel intimidated.

"Mr. Fleming, good to meet you. Thanks for coming to help your friend."

"Yes, she has had quite the course of experiences."

"Let's go into my office to chat a bit before meeting with her and the treatment team. Water, beverage of any kind?" she asked him.

"No thank you, I'm fine."

Her office was modest in size for a masters' level clinician, but comfortable enough for a small family conference or any one-on-one sessions. Her movements were direct and easy, but you could tell she wanted to set a certain tone for the conversation. She had only been at this for four years but had scored well in all clinical and performance reviews. She was good, but not hypervigilant. Her attire was teacher salary basic with a shallow upgrade. She was married with two young kids.

"Mr. Fleming, of course your reputation precedes you, so I will defer, when necessary," she begins.

"Well thank you but I will follow your leading and add where I can."

"Thank you, this is what we have."

Larry was patient as she took fifteen or so minutes to review all relevant permissions, and psych-social history information on Ms. Bishop. The only thing new to him was a reference to her being molested at eleven years old. At some point she had given the staff a name, but it had not been repeated by her. It seemed an obscure reference with no validity. Larry remained silent on that subject and asked about her behavior today.

"She's not well. She's been sitting in the day room talking to herself and moving if anyone tried to sit near her. She did not attend group or recreational therapy. She ate some of her breakfast, and her vitals are stable," the social worker relayed to him.

"What would you have me do?" Larry asked, curious that she had not mentioned Rita's terminal illness.

"She seems to cycle in and out of reality and we would like to make discharge plans but she's not socially stable at his time. We would hope seeing you resets her reality base. When she's lucid she speaks highly of you."

"So further back what's been happening?"

"Well, some days, or parts of days she babbles, and no one can understand what she's talking about, other times she's as clear as a professor on topic. Then she has her sleep over days where she stays in her room and sits in the chair for hours on end, then gets back in bed. Her hygiene suffers during those times."

"Ms. Baker, you've made no reference to her physical diagnosis," he says to her.

"Oh," she pauses and looks over some notes in the chart. "I don't follow you."

"Cancer, she has terminal Brain Cancer. She only has months to live."

"The intake assessment didn't include that, I'm afraid."

"And she's been here how long?" he asks her in a pointed way.

"I know where you're going, I have not done my job."

"Well of course any planning will have to include that. No notes from the attending physician?" Larry asks as he gets heated about this lapse.

"Mr. Fleming, I think I need to be excused," she asks of him, getting up from the chair and going down the hall to the nurse's station. "I'll be right back."

Chapter 7

As he sat Larry thought of the past and one of his first clients.

When Larry's mentor called, he could only tell him that the secret service would be involved, and he needed to be in his office by 7am Thursday morning, and that they would get there early, clean his office before and after the visit. Also, he would need to wear a suit and tie, shoes should be polished. Larry had been a certified addiction counselor only two years at that time. When she walked in security posted down the hall, not in front of the office door, and not in his office lobby. He would be alone with her for an hour.

She was tall, wearing pumps and a crisp linen suit, softly laced blouse, and no handbag. Her makeup was light, and she seemed to be about thirty-five years old. He recognized her right away, and did not reach out to shake her hand, she offered first, and he obliged.

"Mr. Fleming, Joy Winslip, my father sends his regards. He and Nelson are friends since college."

"Thank you, please sit down."

He gestures to the Queen Anne style love seat just beyond his desk, past the single chair. She sits and looks about the office. She seems uncomfortable and moves to the other chair, closer to him. He sits in his swivel and tries not to stare at her; she's gorgeous. She relaxes, crosses her legs, and begins a tale of drug abuse, crime, and a possible indictment. After an hour she asks to see him again next week, same time. He agrees. She gets up, thanks him, and leaves.

Larry quicky calls Mr. Nelson.

"Nelson, Larry. How are you this morning?" he asked his mentor.

"Fine, fine, thanks for calling. How are you?"

"Good, things are good. Ms. Winslip?"

"Okay, good, yes, you're learning. All I'm going to say is be yourself, strip away the excess, that's not your business. That's another world, stick to what you know. Be honest and listen more than talk."

"Okay. Thanks."

The next week she arrives, same as before, but this time a guard stands by the office door, outside in the hall. She takes a seat, and after pleasantries, she cries and starts to talk through the tears.

"How could I have been so stupid. I'm not a young woman, not a teenager. That bastard overdosed, I knew he wasn't strong enough, but the sex, you know, wild. So, he's smoking crack, and I'm shooting heroin, he passes out, drunk. Okay, so, I know, but anyway, I'm here, and they tried to get money from me, a lot. Man, those gang bangers are stupid. I pulled up with security, and they think they're going to rob me, stupid. Anyway, I've been clean a week and I'm okay. Oh, I did go to one of those meetings and it was good. I'm clean today. He didn't die, but he kept calling, I told him to go away. He has some pictures, but I'm not going to worry about that. I'm not the first one, right? I look good with clothes on or naked. Post them, I don't care. No money, bitch. So, you got any suggestions?"

"Do the next right thing."

"Okay, I'll see you next week."

*

Larry had his eyes closed and was in a deep meditative state when the social worker returned with his old friend Dr. Scott. They grinned a slow widening smile when Larry opened his eyes and saw the doctor. Lindsey Baker slowly retreated to a seat behind her desk as the doctor sat in the chair next to Larry.

"It's nice to see you Larry but this is a tough circumstance. The clinical lapse has been corrected and I offer my apologies," the doctor offers to his colleague.

"Thank you, sir. How is Ms. Bishop?" he asks, looking towards Ms. Baker.

"Mr. Fleming, it was a major oversight on my part. That will not happen again with another client of mine. And I appreciate Dr. Scott joining us."

"Yes, her situation is difficult, and we will keep her as comfortable as possible. It may be time for a hospice regimen, and we can do that here in the North Wing of the facility," Dr. Scott speaks up.

"Should we try for a visit today?" Larry asks.

"She is not coherent today, but if you would like to speak to her that would be fine."

"I would like to see her and for her to see me."

"Let's arrange that, in her room?" the doctor directs to Ms. Baker.

"She's out in the dayroom now and I will get her, and you can meet us there Mr. Fleming."

"I would prefer the larger room. Are many other clients there now?" he asks.

"No, about three," she responds and looks to Dr. Scott for guidance.

"I think that will be fine," doctor responds.

*

A copy of Larry's last book, The Moon Is My Confessor, was on a bookshelf in her office when Lindsey Baker came to work at Avery. She had read it and dismissed it as a good piece of fiction that didn't give her much insight into any psychiatric illnesses she had encountered up to that time. She thought it a nice thriller more appropriate for a prison population.

*

It was discovered that Jake had an eighty percent blockage of his circumplex artery and had a stent put in. There was no damage to his heart.

After Rita passed Jake and Leroy decided to donate the gold to the Avery Institute. They named the Mental Health wing after Rita Bishop.

Jake and Marie, Leroy and Celia, and Larry and Stephanie went on about the business of their lives in virtual anonymity.

Also by George H. Clowers, Jr.

All That We Are After
The Writer's Playground: Short Stories
The Moon Is My Confessor
The Case for Larry Fleming
Theft by Taking: A Fictional Memoir
I Wish to Hear the Autumn Wind
A Place, Then Nowhere
If You Have Nothing Better to Do...
I Paint, He Writes: Life Together
Book II and Others
Long Time to Sunset
There Is This Place

Watch for more at https://www.georgeclowers.com.

About the Author

Retired substance use disorder counselor.
Read more at https://www.georgeclowers.com.

9 798227 105028